SAMANTHA BENEKE

The Pet

Contents

Author's Note

Reading Order

The Pet is the first book in the Captive Hearts Series and should be read in sequential order for the best reading experience:

1. The Pet (Book 1)
2. The Partner (Book 2)
3. The One (Book 3)

The Pet is a supernatural vampire romance between a human and her centuries-old vampire art patron, suitable for readers over 18. Content warning: kidnap, forced proximity, blood, sexual intimacy.

Prologue: First Encounter

New York, Three Years Earlier

The Westbrook Gallery in Chelsea had a quiet, hushed atmosphere to it this evening, which Devon Karlov preferred when viewing art. He moved through the space with unhurried ease, hands clasped behind his back, his tall figure cutting a distinguished silhouette against the gallery's stark white walls. His dark suit was meticulously tailored, his presence commanding yet understated.

He hadn't planned to visit this particular gallery today. His schedule in New York was usually filled with meetings related to his various business interests. But something about the promotional flyer he had glimpsed with its splash of violent red against deep midnight blue had drawn him here during a rare free evening.

The exhibition was titled "Fractured Light: New Works by Katherine Morgan," an artist unknown to Devon despite his thorough knowledge of the contemporary art world. This in itself was intriguing; after some time of collecting, few talents emerged that he had not at least heard of through his extensive network.

As he moved deeper into the gallery, the paintings began to affect him in a way he had not experienced in some time. Each work seemed to pulse with raw, visceral emotion. Pain transformed into beauty, alchemized into visual poetry.

Devon stopped before a large canvas dominated by shattered planes of color; fragments of blue and gold that seemed to simultaneously fall apart and come together, creating a tension that was almost physically uncomfortable to look at. Yet he could not look away. The technical skill was clearly there, but it was the emotional content that captivated him. The artist had somehow captured the precise feeling of being broken and remade, of destruction as a prelude to transformation.

"That one's called 'Reconstruction,'" a gallery assistant offered, approaching cautiously, perhaps sensing something in Devon's intense focus that suggested he should not be disturbed. "It's one of Katherine's most recent works."

Devon nodded slightly, never once tearing his gaze from the piece before him. "The artist," he said after a moment, "is she here today?"

"No, sir," the assistant replied. "Ms Morgan rarely attends her own exhibitions. She's quite private about her work."

An artist who let her work speak for itself, that in itself, was interesting.

Near the end of the exhibition, a small table held copies of an art magazine opened to a feature on Katherine Morgan. Devon picked it up, his eyes immediately drawn to a photograph accompanying the article. It captured the artist in profile, standing before what appeared to be a work in progress in her studio.

Her posture was distinctive; arms behind her back as though easing pain from long hours at the canvas, her spine curved slightly with the stance of someone who spent countless hours in focused creation. Her brown hair was tied back in a messy bun, her striped shirt covered in paint stains, which didn't seem to bother her at all.

But it was her expression that Devon found compelling.

She looked up at the work before her with satisfaction, a small smile playing on her lips.

Her green eyes held an almost transcendent, dreamlike quality. It was the look of an artist communing directly with creation, experiencing that rare moment when the work takes on a life of its own, when creator and created exist in perfect harmony.

Devon studied the photograph with an intensity that might have seemed unsettling to an observer. He began to read the article, absorbing details about Katherine Morgan's background; her art education at RISD, her relatively late emergence onto the New York art scene, the critical acclaim that had gradually built around her work despite her reluctance to engage in the social activities of the art world. The writer noted her intensely private nature and her dedication to her craft above all else.

"Morgan rarely discusses the personal experiences that inform her art, preferring to let the work speak for itself."

Devon closed the magazine, his decision made. He approached the gallery director's office, knocking lightly on the open door.

"Mr Karlov," the director greeted him, rising from behind her desk with evident pleasure. They had done business before; Devon was known in certain art circles as a serious collector with impeccable taste and the resources to indulge it. "I didn't know you were visiting today. What do you think of Ms Morgan's work?"

"I'll take all of them," Devon said simply.

The director blinked, momentarily startled despite her professional composure. "All… the entire exhibition?"

"Yes," Devon confirmed, his tone making it clear that he was not given to repeating himself. "And I would appreciate any information you can provide about Ms Morgan's previous work. I may be interested in acquiring pieces from her earlier collections as well."

"Of course," the director replied, recovering quickly. "That's… wonderful news. Ms Morgan will be thrilled. She's been hoping to place her work with serious collectors who appreciate—"

"I would prefer that my identity not be disclosed to the artist at this time," Devon interrupted, his tone polite but firm. "Simply inform her that a private collector has acquired the exhibition."

The director looked momentarily confused but nodded her agreement. In the art world, collector eccentricities were to be accommodated, especially when they came with purchases of this size.

"As you wish, Mr Karlov. I'll prepare the paperwork immediately. Will you be shipping the works to your Budapest residence, or…?"

"Budapest," Devon specified. "I'll have my assistant contact you with the details."

As the director busied herself with the administrative tasks of the transaction, Devon returned to the exhibition space, moving once more through the collection that would soon be his. He stopped again before "Reconstruction" to study the fractured planes of blue and gold.

There was something in Katherine Morgan's work that spoke to him on a level he had not experienced in a very long time, a recognition, perhaps, of a kindred spirit who understood what it meant to be broken and remade, and exist in a state of perpetual reconstruction. Her art revealed a soul that had experienced profound pain yet refused to be defined by it, that transformed trauma into beauty without diminishing its reality.

Devon's gaze returned to the magazine, still open to Katherine Morgan's photograph. He studied the focused intensity in her face again, the moment of communion with her creation. Something stirred within him, an interest that went beyond aesthetic appreciation, beyond the collector's instinct for significant talent.

Devon left the gallery with the transaction complete, stepping out into the bright neon lights of New York. Behind him, Katherine Morgan's paintings waited to be packed and shipped back to Budapest, the first tangible connection between them; she just didn't know it yet.

Moving through the crowded streets, anonymous among the masses of humanity, Devon found himself experiencing something he had not felt in a very long time: Anticipation. Not only for the arrival of the artwork, but for… possibility. A sense that something significant had begun today.

Chapter 1

The gallery was a repurposed warehouse in Budapest's up-and-coming arts district featuring exposed brick walls and polished concrete floors. In the dim light, spotlights shone down creating bright areas that highlighted Kate's paintings and their vibrant bursts of color. The high ceilings and industrial beams gave the space an expansive feel, while the minimalist design ensured nothing competed with the artwork.

Kate Morgan tugged at the sleeve of her black cocktail dress, feeling both overdressed and underdressed for her own exhibition opening. The gallery owner had insisted on formal attire, but Kate would have preferred her paint-splattered jeans and a comfortable sweater. Her dark hair was pulled back in a sleek bun that already threatened to come undone, a few rebellious strands framing her face.

She stood in the corner, a glass of champagne clutched in her hand more as a prop than a beverage. She took in the reactions to her work, but she didn't engage in conversation. Words had never been her strong suit; that's why she painted. Each canvas displayed was a piece of her soul, emotions she could never articulate verbalized through energetic strokes of color and texture.

The Budapest exhibition was a incredible opportunity, one her New York agent had practically forced her to accept. "Eastern European collectors are hungry for American contemporary art," he'd said. "And this particular collector has specifically requested your work." The thought made her uncomfortable, being "requested" like an item on a menu.

Another group of well-dressed patrons approached one of her larger pieces, a chaotic storm of crimson and black that she'd created after her last relationship imploded. Kate felt the familiar tightness in her chest. They were looking at her pain, her heartbreak, her inability to trust. And they were sipping champagne while doing it.

Devon Karlov entered the gallery precisely forty-five minutes after the exhibition opening began, late enough to make an entrance, early enough not to miss anything significant. His tailored black suit was impeccably cut, moving with him like a second skin. At six-foot-two, with aristocratic features and dark hair, he commanded attention without seeking it.

He moved through the gallery with practiced poise, nodding to acquaintances he had cultivated over years. His eyes, however, never left the corner where Kate stood. He could sense her discomfort from across the room, the tension in her shoulders, the way she held herself apart from the crowd. It was familiar to him, that self-protective stance.

He approached her work methodically, spending time with each piece, truly seeing what others simply looked at. When he reached the large crimson and black canvas, he stood motionless before it for several minutes. He recognized the pain that emanated from the desperate brushstrokes. The painting was not just color and texture; it was a scream.

"She won't tell anyone what this one means," came a voice at Devon's elbow. The gallery owner, András, smiled broadly. "Our Ms Morgan guards her interpretations as fiercely as her privacy."

Devon's lips curved slightly. "As she should. Art that explains itself requires no contemplation."

András nodded enthusiastically. "You must meet her. She's just over there, trying very hard to become invisible."

Before Kate could retreat further into her corner, András was leading Devon toward her. She straightened, adopting the polite but distant expression she reserved for these necessary interactions.

"Ms Morgan, I must introduce you to one of our most distinguished collectors. Devon Karlov, Kate Morgan. Mr Karlov owns several galleries across Europe and has been following your work with great interest."

Devon extended his hand, and Kate hesitated just a fraction of a second before taking it. His hand was cool to the touch, his grip firm but not overwhelming.

"Ms Morgan," he said, his voice carrying just a hint of an accent she couldn't place. "Your work is extraordinary. Particularly the piece with the crimson storm. It speaks of a rage that seeks beauty even in its destruction."

Kate's eyes widened slightly. Most patrons commented on her "interesting use of color" or asked if she was "influenced by Pollock." Few ever saw the emotion behind the abstraction.

"That's… perceptive," she managed, withdrawing her hand.

"Not perception. Recognition." Devon's eyes held hers, and for a moment, Kate felt as though he could see past her carefully constructed walls. "We recognize in others what we know in ourselves."

András, sensing the intensity of the moment, excused himself to greet new arrivals.

"And what is it you think you recognize, Mr Karlov?" Kate asked, her voice steadier than she felt.

Devon smiled, a genuine expression that softened his aristocratic features. "The understanding that the world will always disappoint you, so it's safer to expect nothing."

Kate felt a chill run down her spine. Not because he was wrong, but because he was right.

The musicians in the corner began a new piece, something classical that Kate vaguely recognized but couldn't name. Devon tilted his head slightly, listening.

"Chopin," he said, as if reading her thoughts. "'Aeolian Harp', though adapted for strings. Do you dance, Ms Morgan?"

Kate almost laughed. "Not if I can help it."

"A shame," Devon replied, his eyes never leaving hers. "Movement can be as expressive as brushstrokes."

"I express myself quite enough on canvas, thank you."

"And yet," Devon said, extending his hand, "sometimes we discover new perspectives when we step outside our comfort zones."

Kate looked at his outstretched hand, then back to his face. There was a challenge there, but also something else, understanding, perhaps. Before she could talk herself out of it, she placed her champagne glass on a nearby table and took his hand.

"One dance," she said firmly. "And then you'll stop analyzing me."

Devon's smile widened as he led her to the small area where a few couples were already moving to the music. "I make no promises."

His hand settled at the small of her back, respectful but confident. Kate had expected awkwardness; it had been years since she'd danced with anyone. But Devon led with such assurance that she found herself following without thought. Despite maintaining proper distance between them, there was an intimacy in the way he guided her, anticipating her movements before she made them.

"You're surprisingly good at this," Kate admitted as he turned her smoothly.

"I've had a lot of practice," Devon replied. "One accumulates certain skills over time."

"And what other skills would those be, Mr Karlov?"

"Devon, please." His hand pressed slightly firmer against her back as he guided her through a more complex turn. "I play the piano. I speak several languages. And I can tell when someone is hiding behind their art."

Kate stiffened slightly. "I'm not hiding."

"Aren't you?" His voice was gentle, rather than accusative. "Your paintings reveal what you cannot say. What really inspired your 'Fractured Light'? Is it simply an artistic concept or something more... personal?"

Kate's steps faltered slightly. He was very observant, his comment landing too close to home. "Art is always personal, Mr Karlov," she deflected, her voice tight.

He tilted his head. "Maybe, but some art shows more pain than others. Your crimson storm, for instance. It reflects an old wound that just won't heal."

The music surrounded them, and Kate felt herself getting closer to him. Their bodies were now just inches apart. "Maybe some things aren't meant to be said."

"Or maybe," Devon replied, "they're waiting for the right person to hear them."

They moved in silence for a moment, the rhythm of the music filling the space between them. Kate was acutely aware of his hand in hers, the coolness of his touch, the strength in his fingers.

"What happened to make you stop trusting?" Devon asked suddenly.

Kate nearly missed a step. "That's presumptuous. You don't know me."

"I know your art," Devon replied. "And art never lies, even when the artist does."

The music was drawing to a close, and Kate felt both relief and a strange disappointment. As they slowed their movements, Devon spoke again, his voice lower.

"I know what it's like to put your trust in the wrong hands, and never view the world or others quite the same way again." he said, the words so unexpected that Kate's eyes snapped back to his.

The vulnerability in his admission caught her off guard. Before she could respond, the music ended, and Devon stepped back, releasing her but maintaining eye contact.

"Thank you for the dance, Ms Morgan."

"Kate," she corrected, surprising herself.

His smile returned. "Kate, I would like to propose something," Devon continued, his eyes never leaving hers. "I'm hosting a private viewing at my estate outside the city tomorrow evening. A small gathering of serious collectors and artists. I'd be honored if you would attend."

Kate's instinct was to refuse immediately. She didn't do "private viewings" at strangers' estates. But something in his understanding of her work, and now this glimpse of shared experience, made her hesitate.

"Your work deserves to be seen by people who truly understand it," he added, as if sensing her reluctance. "Not just those who wish to hang something striking in their dining rooms"

Despite herself, Kate felt a smile tugging at her lips. "You seem very confident that you understand my work, Devon."

He produced a business card from his jacket pocket, offering it to her. "And I don't claim to understand it completely. That's what makes it fascinating."

Kate took the card, noting the embossed lettering and the address of his gallery.

"The car would collect you at seven," he said. "Unless you prefer to make your own way.

"I haven't said yes," Kate pointed out.

Devon smiled again, and this time there was something almost predatory in it, though gone so quickly she might have imagined it. "You haven't said no, either."

Before she could respond, he nodded politely. "Think about it. My number is on the card." With that, he moved away, leaving Kate staring after him, the business card still in her hand.

* * *

The gallery suddenly felt too warm, too crowded. Kate slipped the business card into her clutch and made her way toward the exit, nodding politely to patrons who tried to engage her. She needed air, space to think.

Outside, the cool night air was a relief. Kate leaned against the brick wall of the gallery, closing her eyes briefly. The dance with Devon replayed in her mind. His perceptiveness, the unexpected connection, the way he seemed to understand her work on a level few others did. His invitation to the estate lingered in her thoughts.

"Maybe," she whispered to herself. Despite all her instincts warning caution, she was tempted. Not just by the professional opportunity, but by the man himself. There was something compelling about Devon Karlov, something that had broken through her carefully maintained defences.

A sound from the alley beside the gallery interrupted her thoughts, a muffled cry, quickly silenced. Kate frowned, pushing away from the wall. Probably nothing, but...

She moved cautiously toward the alley entrance, peering around the corner. In the dim light, she could make out two figures. One pressed against the wall, the other bent over them. At first, she thought she was witnessing a romantic encounter, but something felt wrong. The stillness of the person against the wall, the predatory stance of the other.

Kate took another step, and her heel clicked against the pavement. The standing figure turned sharply, and Kate's breath caught in her throat.

Devon Karlov straightened, his mouth stained with red. The person against the wall, a young woman in server's attire from the gallery, slumped slightly, her eyes glazed. A thin trail of blood trickled down her neck.

For a moment, time seemed suspended. Devon's eyes, now unnaturally bright blue, locked with Kate's. Recognition, then something like regret flashed across his features.

"Kate," he said, his voice perfectly calm despite the blood on his lips.

Terror shot through her like electricity. Kate backed away, then turned and ran, her heart hammering in her chest. Behind her, she heard Devon call her name again, but she didn't stop. She fled toward the street, toward people and light and safety, the business card burning in her clutch like a brand.

The private viewing invitation now took on a sinister new meaning. And yet, even as fear propelled her forward, a part of her mind couldn't connect the monster in the alley with the man who had danced with her, who had shared his own vulnerability, who had seen through her art to the pain beneath.

Kate hailed a taxi with shaking hands, giving the driver her hotel address. As the car pulled away from the curb, she glanced back at the gallery entrance. Devon stood there, composed once more, watching her departure with an unreadable expression.

She had been right all along. Never believe the best in people.

Chapter 2

Kate's hotel room was elegant but impersonal with crisp white bedding, and tasteful artwork that she hadn't bothered to really look at. The kind of room that could be anywhere in the world. After fleeing the gallery, she had rushed through the lobby, ignoring the concierge's greeting, and locked herself in her room, double-checking the deadbolt and security chain.

Now, hours later, she sat on the edge of the bed, still in her black cocktail dress, though she'd kicked off her heels the moment she entered. Her hands had finally stopped shaking, but her mind wouldn't quiet. The image of Devon Karlov, sophisticated, perceptive Devon, with blood on his lips and that inhuman brightness in his eyes, kept replaying in her head.

Kate pushed herself up from the bed and moved to the minibar, extracting a tiny bottle of whiskey. She didn't bother with a glass, just twisted the cap off and took a burning swallow. The alcohol did little to calm her racing thoughts.

Vampire. The word seemed absurd, something from horror movies and teenage fiction. And yet, what else could explain what she'd seen? The woman's glazed eyes, the blood, Devon's unnatural blue eyes when he'd turned toward her…

She took another swallow of whiskey and moved to the window, pushing aside the heavy curtain to look down at the Budapest street below. The city lights blurred through the glass, beautiful and distant. She should call someone—her agent, the police, the American embassy. But what would she say? That she'd witnessed a vampire feeding? That the collector who'd been so interested in her work, who'd danced with her and seemed to understand her, was some kind of monster?

Kate let the curtain fall back into place and leaned against the glass, closing her eyes and taking a deep breath. Maybe she'd imagined it. The stress of the exhibition, the unexpected connection with Devon, the champagne, perhaps it had all combined to create some kind of hallucination.

But she knew better. What she'd seen had been real.

She finished the whiskey and tossed the empty bottle into the trash. Her phone lay on the nightstand, and she picked it up, scrolling through her contacts. Her finger hovered over her agent's name, but she hesitated. What was she going to do, demand an immediate flight home because a collector turned out to be a vampire? She'd sound insane.

Instead, she set an alarm for early morning. She'd change her flight then, get out of Budapest as quickly as possible. For now, she needed sleep. The adrenaline crash was hitting her hard, leaving her limbs heavy and her thoughts sluggish.

Kate didn't bother with her usual nighttime routine. She simply stripped off her dress, pulled on an oversized t-shirt she slept in, and crawled under the covers. Despite her racing mind, exhaustion pulled her quickly toward sleep.

Her last conscious thought was of Devon's eyes during their dance, before she knew what he was, and how they had seemed to see straight through her carefully constructed walls.

* * *

Kate wasn't sure how long she had been asleep when something pulled her awake. The faint glow of city lights filtered through the curtains and at some point during the night it had started to rain. The sound of it pattering against the window created a soothing rhythm.

She blinked slowly, still half-asleep, watching the raindrops trickle down the window in silvery trails, illuminated by the streetlight outside. The shadows in the room shifted and moved with the rain's patterns, creating an almost hypnotic effect.

Then one shadow detached from the others.

Kate's drowsiness vanished in an instant as she saw the distinctly human silhouette move across the light. She bolted upright in bed with a gasp, her heart hammering against her ribs.

Before she could scream, a cool hand clamped over her mouth, pushing her back down onto the mattress. Another hand pinned her shoulder, the grip firm but not painful.

"Please don't scream," came Devon's voice, low and controlled. "I'm not going to hurt you."

In the darkness Kate could make out his features above her. He looked exactly as he had at the gallery, elegant and composed, except for the intensity in his eyes. There was no blood on his lips now, no visible sign of the creature she'd seen in the alley. But she knew what he was.

Her heart raced so fast she felt lightheaded, but she managed a small nod. Slowly, Devon removed his hand from her mouth, though he maintained his hold on her shoulder.

"How did you get in here?" she whispered, her voice unsteady.

A faint smile touched his lips. "Hotel security is designed to keep humans out."

The casual confirmation of his inhuman nature sent a fresh wave of fear through her. Kate pressed herself deeper into the mattress, as if she could somehow sink through it and escape.

"This isn't how I wanted things to begin," Devon said, his voice carrying a note of genuine regret. "The exhibition, the private viewing at my estate, it was all meant to happen gradually. You weren't supposed to see… what you saw in the alley."

"What are you?" Kate asked, though she already knew the answer.

Devon studied her face for a moment before responding. "I think you've already figured that out."

"Vampire," she whispered, the word feeling ridiculous even as she said it. He inclined his head slightly, neither confirming nor denying, but his silence was answer enough. "What do you want from me?" Kate asked, surprised by the steadiness in her voice.

Devon's expression softened, and he released her shoulder, though he remained poised above her. "That," he said, "is a loaded question with infinite answers." His eyes traveled over her face, lingering on her lips. "But for now, perhaps a kiss would suffice?

The request was so unexpected, so at odds with the situation, that Kate could only gape at him in disbelief, her mouth wide open. Yet as he leaned closer, she felt a bewildering mixture of fear and something else. A pull, a curiosity, a need she couldn't explain. His cool breath fanned across her face, and despite everything she knew, everything she'd seen, she didn't turn away.

Their lips were inches apart when Devon's hand moved to her neck. His fingers found a pressure point with practiced skill, and Kate felt a sudden numbness spread from that spot. Her vision blurred, her limbs became heavy, and the last thing she saw before losing consciousness was Devon's intense blue eyes, watching her with a complicated mix of regret and determination.

Devon caught Kate as she went limp, supporting her head as it fell back against the pillow. For a moment, he simply looked at her, his expression unreadable. Then, with efficient movements, he gathered her belongings. He placed everything in her suitcase, her phone, passport, a few clothes from the closet and her toiletries from the bathroom.

Moving to the door, Devon unlocked and opened it slightly to make brief eye contact with the night maintenance worker he had compelled earlier that evening. The man's eyes held the glassy, distant look of someone under compulsion as Devon handed him the suitcase.

"Service entrance. Black car," Devon said quietly. The compelled worker nodded and disappeared down the hallway without a word, his movements mechanical, but purposeful.

Devon closed the door and returned to the task at hand. From his pocket, he withdrew an envelope containing cash in euros to cover the room, which he left on the desk with a note instructing the hotel that Ms Morgan had been called away unexpectedly and would not be returning.

Returning to the bed, Devon wrapped Kate in the hotel bathrobe, then lifted her effortlessly into his arms Her head lolled against his shoulder, dark hair spilling over his arm. He stood for a moment, looking down at her face, relaxed in unconsciousness.

"This isn't how I wanted it to begin," he murmured, though she couldn't hear him. "But sometimes fate forces our hand."

With Kate secure in his arms, Devon moved to the balcony door he had entered through, sliding it open once again. The rain had intensified, drumming against the concrete balcony and the city beyond. He stepped out into the downpour, unmindful of the water soaking through his clothes and Kate's robe.

Below, a black car idled at the service entrance, its engine a quiet purr in the night. Devon looked once more at Kate's face, then stepped onto the balcony railing. Without hesitation, he stepped off, dropping six floors with Kate in his arms, landing with inhuman grace on the pavement below. The car door opened as he approached. Devon placed Kate gently on the back seat, then slid in beside her, pulling her head onto his lap.

"Home," he told the driver, who nodded without a word. The car left the hotel and moved into the rainy night in Budapest. Devon softly stroked Kate's hair, keeping his eyes on the city lights outside the window. "You'll understand eventually," he said quietly. "Some cages are built to protect, not to imprison."

As the words left his lips, he wondered whether he was trying to convince her or himself.

Chapter 3

Kate woke up in a room filled with soft, diffused light. Heavy curtains were drawn over what Kate thought were windows, letting in a faint glow around their edges. The space was bigger than her whole New York apartment, featuring a large four-poster bed and graceful antique furniture along the walls. A sitting area with a small sofa and armchairs occupied one corner, and three doors led to what she could only guess were a bathroom, a closet, and an exit. Despite the luxury surrounding her, the room had the unmistakable feeling of a cage, albeit a gilded one.

Consciousness returned to Kate in fragments, first sensation, then sound, finally sight. The silk sheets felt cool against her skin, the mattress impossibly comfortable beneath her. Her head throbbed dully, a lingering effect of whatever Devon had done to knock her out. For a moment, disorientation clouded her mind, her surroundings unfamiliar and dreamlike.

Then memory crashed back; the gallery, the alley, Devon in her hotel room, his fingers at her neck. Kate sat up straight, her heart pounding in her chest. She was no longer in the oversized t-shirt she'd worn to sleep at the hotel. Instead, she wore a silk nightgown that was unfamiliar to her. The thought that someone, possibly Devon, had changed her clothes filled her with a sense of violation.

"Where am I?" she whispered to the empty room. Her voice sounded small and fragile in the vast space. There was movement in the corner of the room, a figure sat in one of the armchairs, partially hidden in shadow. As her eyes adjusted, the silhouette resolved into Devon Karlov, watching her with an unreadable expression. He was dressed in dark trousers and a charcoal sweater that somehow managed to look both comfortable and expensive.

"You're in my home," Devon said, his voice calm and measured. "About an hour outside Budapest."

Kate instinctively pulled the duvet up to her chest, as if the fabric could shield her from him. "You kidnapped me," she said, her voice steadier than she felt.

"I removed you from a situation that had become untenable," Devon corrected, rising from the chair with effortless grace. He moved toward the bed but stopped at a respectful distance, seeming to sense her fear. "What you saw at the gallery complicated matters."

"Complicated matters?" Kate repeated incredulously. "I saw you drinking someone's blood!"

Devon's expression didn't change. "Yes."

The simple acknowledgment hung in the air between them. Kate had half-expected denial, explanations, excuses, anything but this calm acceptance of what he was.

"You're a vampire," she said, the word still feeling ridiculous despite everything.

"That's the term humans have settled on, yes." Devon moved to the window and drew back the heavy curtains, revealing that it was night outside. Through the glass, Kate could see manicured gardens illuminated by subtle landscape lighting. "Though like most labels, it fails to capture the complexity of the reality."

Kate's mind raced, searching for a way out of this nightmare. The door was across the room, past Devon. Even if she could somehow get past him, where would she go? She had no idea where she was, no phone, no money.

"Why am I here?" she asked, trying to keep her voice from trembling. "What do you want from me?"

Devon turned from the window to face her, his expression softening slightly. "I've been following your work for three years, Kate. Since I first saw one of your paintings in a small gallery in SoHo. The raw emotion in your brushstrokes, the way you transform pain into beauty, it spoke to me in a way few things have in my long existence."

"So you're what, an art enthusiast who kidnaps artists he admires?" Kate's fear was giving way to anger, a safer emotion to cling to.

A faint smile touched Devon's lips. "Not typically, no. You're… an exception."

"Lucky me," Kate muttered.

Devon moved to the sitting area and gestured to the armchair opposite the one he'd been occupying. "Would you join me? This conversation might be more comfortable if you're not cowering in bed."

Kate hesitated, weighing her options. Remaining in bed felt vulnerable, but moving closer to Devon seemed dangerous. After a moment, she slid from beneath the covers, relieved to find the nightgown was modest enough. She found a throw blanket at the foot of the bed and placed it over her shoulders, then cautiously approached the sitting area. Instead of taking the offered chair, she perched on the edge of the sofa, maintaining maximum distance between them. Devon nodded slightly, as if acknowledging her choice, and returned to his own seat.

"I had planned to court you properly," he said, the antiquated phrasing catching Kate off guard. "The exhibition, the invitation to my estate, it was all meant to happen gradually, to give you time to know me before…"

"Before I discovered you're a monster?" Kate finished.

Devon's eyes flashed with something, hurt? Anger? It was gone too quickly to identify. "Before you discovered I'm not human," he corrected. "There's a difference."

"Not from where I'm sitting."

"Fair enough." Devon leaned back in his chair, studying her. "What you saw in the alley was… unfortunate. I don't typically feed so carelessly, but the evening had been… affecting. Dancing with you, the connection I felt, it heightened certain appetites."

Kate shuddered at the implication. "Is she dead? The server?"

"No," Devon replied immediately. "She's perfectly fine, if missing a few memories of our encounter. I never kill when I feed, Kate. That would be both wasteful and unnecessarily cruel."

"How considerate of you," Kate said bitterly. "And what about me? Am I here to be your next meal?"

Devon's expression darkened. "If that were my intention, we wouldn't be having this conversation."

The silence that followed was heavy with unspoken threats and fears. Kate pulled the blanket tighter around her shoulders.

"Then why am I here?" she asked again, her voice smaller now.

Devon leaned forward, his eyes intent on hers. "Because in four centuries of existence, I've never encountered anyone whose pain so perfectly mirrors my own. Your art screams with the same rage I've carried since my maker held me captive and used me as a puppet for decades."

The personal revelation caught Kate off guard. She remembered his words during their dance about having his own trust broken.

"So this is what? Therapy? You kidnapped me because my art speaks to your trauma?"

"Consider my estate a sanctuary," Devon corrected. "For both of us. A place where two damaged souls might find understanding."

Kate laughed, the sound harsh and disbelieving. "Sanctuary? You abducted me and now you're holding me prisoner. That's not a sanctuary, Devon. That's captivity."

"For now," he acknowledged. "Until you understand that I mean you no harm. That I can offer you something few others can, true understanding comprehension of the pain you express in your art."

Kate stood abruptly, the blanket falling from her shoulders. "I want to go home."

Devon remained seated, his posture relaxed despite the tension between them. "That's not possible at the moment."

"You can't keep me here against my will!"

"I think we've established that I can," Devon replied calmly.

"People will be looking for me!" Kate said desperately. "My agent, my family, they'll know something's wrong when I don't check in."

Devon's expression remained infuriatingly calm. "I'm afraid they won't. My team has been quite thorough in managing your digital presence. Your agent received an email this morning informing her that you've accepted an unexpected artist residency outside Budapest for the foreseeable future. Your family has seen similar updates on your social media, you're apparently thriving in your new creative environment, completely absorbed in your work."

The blood drained from Kate's face. "You hacked my accounts?"

"Among other precautions," Devon confirmed. "Your phone has been responding to messages appropriately, maintaining your established communication patterns. To the outside world, Katherine Morgan is exactly where she wants to be; pursuing her art in an inspiring European setting, too immersed in her work for regular contact."

Kate felt the walls of her cage closing in even tighter. Not only was she physically trapped, but Devon had systematically severed her connections to the outside world. No one would be looking for her because no one knew she was missing.

"You've thought of everything," she whispered, the fight draining out of her voice.

"I've had considerable practice in managing… delicate situations," Devon replied. "But I'd prefer your stay to be as comfortable as possible. This suite is yours. You'll find clothes in the closet. I had your measurements taken while you were unconscious and ordered a suitable wardrobe."

Kate wrapped her arms around herself, feeling exposed. "How thoughtful."

"The bathroom is fully stocked with everything you might need," Devon continued, ignoring her sarcasm. "There's a sitting room through that door—" he gestured to one of the three doors "—with books, a television, and a tablet. The tablet has no external communication capabilities, but it does have access to streaming services and a curated digital library."

"And the third door?" Kate asked, glancing at the remaining exit.

"That leads to the main house. It's locked from the outside."

Of course it was. Kate sank back onto the sofa, the reality of her situation settling over her like a weight. "How long do you intend to keep me here?"

Devon stood, smoothing invisible wrinkles from his sweater. "That depends largely on you, Kate. I have no desire to be your jailer indefinitely. But I can't risk you exposing what I am, either."

"So I'm never leaving."

"I didn't say that." Devon moved toward the door to the main house, then paused. "You'll find that I can be quite reasonable. Earn my trust, and your circumstances will improve accordingly."

"And how exactly am I supposed to do that?" Kate asked, bitterness seeping into her voice.

Devon turned back to her, his expression softening. "For now? Simply try to understand that not all cages are designed to punish. Some are built to protect."

"Protect who? You or me?"

"Perhaps both." Devon reached for the door handle. "You should rest. We'll talk more tomorrow evening."

"Wait," Kate called as he began to open the door. "What am I supposed to do all day while you're… wherever it is you go during daylight?"

A small smile touched Devon's lips. "Sleep, if you wish. Read. Watch films There's also an art studio adjacent to the sitting room, fully stocked with supplies. I thought you might want to continue your work."

The mention of art, her passion and outlet, sent a confusing mix of emotions through Kate. Anger that he presumed to know what she needed, gratitude for the consideration, fear that he understood her so well.

"I've left instructions with the staff to bring you meals at regular intervals," Devon continued.

"They won't enter without knocking, and you're free to refuse them entry if you wish. Though I wouldn't recommend starving yourself out of spite."

"Your concern is touching," Kate said flatly.

Devon inclined his head slightly. "Good night, Kate. I hope you'll use this time to reflect on our situation with an open mind."

Before she could respond, he slipped through the door. Kate heard the unmistakable sound of a lock clicking from the other side. Alone in the luxurious prison, Kate studied her surroundings again. The opulent furnishings, the thoughtful amenities, and the promise of an art studio were all designed to make her captivity more palatable. To seduce her into acceptance.

She moved to the window and pressed her palm against the glass. It was thick, probably reinforced, and the drop to the gardens below was considerable. No escape there.

As she turned away from the window, her eye caught a painting on the wall she hadn't noticed before. With a start, she recognized it as one of her own, a small piece she'd sold to a gallery in New York two years ago. Devon had owned her art long before he owned her.

The realization sent a chill through her. This wasn't a spontaneous abduction; it was the culmination of years of obsession. And somewhere in the massive estate beyond her locked door, a vampire who believed they shared the same pain was waiting for her to accept her gilded cage.

Kate sank onto the edge of the bed, her mind racing with fear, confusion, and the faintest, most troubling hint of curiosity about the man, the creature, who had gone to such lengths to possess her. After a moment, she forced herself to move to the bathroom, needing to wash away the lingering feeling of violation. The bathroom was as opulent as the bedroom, with marble floors and a deep soaking tub.

Opening the cabinets, she found them stocked with high-end toiletries, including her own personal favorites. Devon had anticipated her every need, even the most intimate ones. Kate closed the drawer with trembling fingers, unsure whether to feel grateful for the consideration or violated by the intimate knowledge of her needs.

Chapter 4

Morning light filtered through the heavy curtains, painting the opulent suite in soft hues. After a restless night, Kate gave up any attempts of decent sleep. The room, less intimidating in daylight, still felt like a cage, the locked door a constant, stark reminder of her captivity.

She moved through the space, taking stock. She opened a cupboard to find clothing in her size and in styles she might have chosen herself. The unsettling precision of Devon's knowledge, his meticulous planning, sent a shiver down her spine. She chose jeans and a simple sweater, finding a small measure of control in the familiar fabric.

The marble-tiled bathroom offered no solace. She splashed cold water on her face, avoiding her reflection, unwilling to confront the fear in her eyes.

Two doors were left. One, she knew, led to the main house, locked. The other, Devon had mentioned, opened into a sitting room. Taking a deep breath, she turned the handle. The sitting room was spacious, filled with plush sofas, bookshelves, and a large television. A tablet sat on a side table. But it was the slightly ajar door on the far side that caught her attention. Cautiously, she pushed it open.

Sunlight streamed through skylights and tall windows, illuminating a space that stole her breath. An artist's studio, larger and better equipped than any she had ever dreamed of. Easels stood ready, shelves stocked with paints, brushes and tools she had only read about. In the center of the room was a large worktable, ready and waiting. A smaller table beside it held a selection of palette knives.

Kate moved through the space, her fingers trailing over supplies. This was her sanctuary, her voice, her anchor in a chaotic world. And Devon had provided it. A beautiful trap, designed to seduce her into accepting her captivity. He knew all too well how to tempt her.

"Asshole," she muttered. She wouldn't give him the satisfaction of creating art for his pleasure. But her fingers itched. Art had always been her way of processing emotions, her escape. The urge to create beckoned more powerfully than ever now she was trapped.

She turned away, closing the studio door firmly. She wouldn't surrender so easily. But the pull of that room, the promise of release it offered, frightened her almost as much as Devon himself.

Over the next few days, Kate established a rigid routine, a desperate attempt to reclaim some semblance of control. Mornings involved carefully looking for ways to escape. She examined reinforced windows, strong locks, and sturdy walls. Each unsuccessful attempt weakened her determination, filling her with a deep sense of defeat. Breakfast came at 8:00 AM, brought by a quiet woman who provided no information, no connection, and no hope. Kate quickly learned the staff were well-instructed, their efficiency a cold, polite wall. She was truly alone.

By afternoon, she found herself drawn back to the studio, like a magnet. She simply sat at first, taking in the light from the large windows. On day three she unwrapped a pencil and sketchbook, her fingers caressing the wooden stem, resisting the urge to press it into paper. On the fourth day, she prepared and stretched a canvas. By the fifth, she was painting furiously and desperately. Colors filled the canvas in raw expressions of her rage and fear. She painted until the light started to fade, marking Devon's waking hours.

As twilight approached, she would clean her brushes, cover her work, and retreat to her bedroom, washing away the evidence of her surrender to the studio's temptation. Dinner arrived at 7:00 PM, eaten quickly behind a locked door, a futile, yet defiant gesture.

Devon arrived each evening with a polite knock at the door. He made small talk, and she replied with brief answers. Their interactions felt tense. He never mentioned her art, but she suspected he visited the studio while she was away to watch her progress. The idea made her uneasy.

She stayed awake as late as possible, reading or watching films on the tablet, only allowing herself to sleep when she was certain dawn was approaching. Her routine was a delicate shield. It aimed to reduce contact and preserve her sanity through creative expression.

Then she discovered the gardens.

On her seventh day, Kate saw a glass door in the art studio that was partially hidden. It was unlocked. The door opened onto a private terrace, which led down stone steps to the estate gardens. She stood frozen, hardly believing what she saw. Was it an oversight, or another test?

The lure of fresh air was too strong. She stepped outside and felt the afternoon sun warm her face for the first time in a week. The gardens stretched out before her, well-kept and filled with blooms. Stone pathways wound through the formal hedges, leading deeper into the area. She wandered for nearly an hour, exploring the grounds and noting the high, unscalable stone wall. Even this freedom had its boundaries.

As the path curved around ancient oak trees, she found a secluded clearing with a stone fire pit and comfortable outdoor furniture. It was bathed in the afternoon sun with views of the distant hills. Kate sank onto a cushioned chair, tilting her face to the sun. For the first time since her abduction, she felt something a little close to peace.

* * *

She hadn't meant to fall asleep. But the sun, the comfort and the emotional exhaustion of the past week were the perfect recipe for rest. The shadows lengthened as she slept, the sun dipping beyond the horizon.

Déjà vu washed over Devon as he ran his fingers through Kate's hair. He remembered the cold, clinical efficiency with which he himself had been taken, not from a hotel room, but from a bustling marketplace in 17th-century Vienna.

He had been a musician then in the household of a minor noble, admired for his skills. He had been content in his station. Until he met Elisabeta, his maker, an ancient creature of terrifying power. She had turned him with calculated cruelty, "offering" him a twisted gift that had plunged him into an abyss of never ending hunger.

The first few decades of his vampiric existence had been a blur of violence. He desperately struggled against the monstrous urges that threatened to consume him. It had taken centuries to master discipline, and build the intricate layers of control that now defined him.

He had learned to feed with precision, to exert his will over others without resorting to brute force, to navigate the human world with a detached elegance that disguised the predator beneath.

He had sworn then, in the depths of his despair, that he would never condemn someone to the eternal struggle he had endured. Yet, here he was, with Kate, a human he had come to desire with an intensity that rivaled his ancient thirst.

He had planned a slow seduction, a gradual unveiling of his world, a choice freely given. But Kate's accidental glimpse into his true nature had shattered his carefully constructed timeline.

He couldn't risk her exposing him, couldn't risk her fear turning into outright hatred. And he couldn't, for the life of him, let her go.

Kate slowly began to wake with the soft lavender of twilight. Then, the sensation of fingers gently stroking her hair. Her eyes flew open. Her head rested in Devon's lap. He sat perfectly still, his expression one of peaceful contemplation.

"Good evening," he said softly. "You seemed so peaceful, I couldn't bear to wake you."

Horror and violation crashed through Kate's momentary disorientation. She scrambled away, nearly falling from the chair. "Don't touch me," she choked out, her voice raw.

Devon remained seated, his hands now resting on his thighs. "I apologize," he said, sounding sincere. "I found you sleeping here and was concerned about the dropping temperature. I should have woken you instead."

Kate wrapped her arms around herself, suddenly aware of the chill. "How long were you watching me sleep?" she demanded, revulsion in her voice.

"Not long," Devon replied. "I've only been awake for about an hour."

The casual reminder of his inhuman nature sent another shiver through her. While she had basked in the sun, he had been dormant. Now he was here, invading even this small piece of freedom.

"I've been exploring your work in the studio," Devon said, changing the subject. "Your new pieces are… powerful. The emotion in them is raw, unfiltered. Even more so than your previous work."

Kate felt exposed. The canvases were pure emotion. Rage, fear, desperation. Private. "Those aren't for you," she said, low and tight.

"Art, once created, belongs to those who experience it," Devon replied. "But I understand your feeling of invasion. I should have asked permission."

"Like you asked permission before abducting me? Before changing my clothes? Before watching me sleep and touching me without consent?" Kate's voice rose, fear transforming into anger.

Devon had the grace to look discomfited. "I've handled this situation poorly," he admitted. "My intentions were good, but my methods…" He sighed. "I'm not accustomed to considering others' feelings. It's been a long time."

"That's not an excuse," Kate said flatly.

"No," Devon agreed. "It's not."

They sat in silence as darkness settled. Lights along the pathways activated, illuminating their faces. In the soft glow, Devon looked almost human. It would be easy to forget what he was. Kate refused to forget.

"I'm going back to my room," she said, standing.

Devon rose. "I'll walk with you."

"I'd rather you didn't."

"The paths can be confusing in the dark," he said.

"I'll manage," Kate replied coldly.

Devon nodded. "As you wish. But may I show you something first? It will only take a moment."

Kate hesitated, suspicion fighting with curiosity.

"Please," Devon added, a genuine note in his voice.

She relented. "Fine. One moment."

* * *

Devon led her along the garden path, keeping a respectful distance. They walked in silence until they reached a small structure Kate hadn't noticed during her exploration, a glass-walled pavilion nestled among flowering trees. Inside, illuminated by subtle lighting, was a grand piano.

"My private sanctuary," Devon said, opening the door and gesturing for her to enter. "As the studio is yours."

Kate stepped inside cautiously. The pavilion was simple but elegant, the piano its centerpiece. "You mentioned during our dance that you play," Kate said, the memory of that evening, before she knew what he was, surfacing unexpectedly.

"It's how I express what I cannot say," Devon replied, echoing her own relationship with painting without realizing it. "Much as you do with your art." He went to the piano but didn't sit down, but instead lightly ran his fingers over the keys with respect. "I thought perhaps…" he began, then paused. "I thought showing you this might help explain why I provided the studio. It wasn't meant as a bribe or a way to win you over, though I can see how it could look like that. It was my way of recognizing a need that I also have."

"Playing piano doesn't make you less of a monster," she said, her voice hard. "And providing an art studio doesn't make you less of a kidnapper."

Devon's expression shuttered, the momentary openness replaced by careful neutrality. "No," he agreed. "It doesn't." He stepped away from the piano, gesturing toward the door. "I've kept you long enough. You know the way back to your suite?"

Kate nodded, relieved that he wasn't insisting on accompanying her.

"Dinner will be delivered at the usual time," Devon said, his tone formal once more. "Good night, Kate."

She left without responding, following the illuminated path back toward her suite. Behind her, she heard the soft opening notes of Chopin's Aeolian Harp, the piece they had danced to at the gallery. The music followed her through the garden, hauntingly beautiful and achingly sad.

Kate quickened her pace, trying to outrun both the music and the unwelcome empathy it stirred within her.

Chapter 5

Two weeks had passed since Kate arrived at Devon's estate. Two weeks of carefully maintained routine, a shield against the unsettling reality of her captivity. She woke with the dawn, retreated to her room at dusk, and spent maximum time in the art studio, a sanctuary Devon had so cunningly provided.

But nature had other plans.

The storm began in the late afternoon, dark clouds gathering with ominous speed. Kate was in the art studio, working on a canvas thrashed with swift, angry strokes of color, some painted by brush, others with her bare hands. Through the skylights, she watched the approaching darkness with growing unease.

Thunder rumbled, and the first fat raindrops spattered against the glass. Within minutes, a deluge hammered against the roof and windows. Lightning flashed, illuminating the studio in stark white, followed by a deafening crack of thunder. The lights flickered, then died, plunging the studio into premature twilight.

Kate stood frozen, paintbrush in hand. The seconds stretched into minutes. No backup generator. A new anxiety gripped her: without power, the electronic locks on her suite doors would default to their fail-safe mode, locked. She could be trapped in the studio as night fell, as Devon awakened.

She set down her brush and wiped her hands. She needed to get back to her bedroom, to the relative safety of her locked door. The thought of him finding her alone in the darkened studio, vulnerable, sent a shiver down her spine.

She navigated carefully through the dim studio to the sitting room. It was even darker, its windows heavily curtained. She found the door to her bedroom and turned the handle. It didn't move. Locked.

"No, no, no," Kate muttered, jiggling the handle uselessly. Trapped. Cut off from her sanctuary just as night was falling.

Another flash of lightning, another thunderclap. The storm intensified, and with it, Kate's sense of exposure. She retreated to the studio, where fading daylight offered some visibility. Perhaps the garden door? A desperate plan, but better than waiting.

As she reached for the handle, a voice spoke from the shadows. "The entire security system is down. You won't get far."

Kate whirled around. Devon stood in the doorway, his silhouette outlined by a flash of lightning. He was dressed casually, his hair slightly damp.

"How long have you been standing there?" Kate demanded, hating the tremor in her voice.

"I just arrived," Devon replied, stepping further into the studio. "The power failure triggered alerts. I came to ensure you were safe."

"I'm fine," Kate said stiffly. "Just locked out of my bedroom."

Another lightning flash, another thunderclap. The storm showed no signs of retreating.

"The staff is working to restore power," Devon said, moving closer. "But the main transformer was struck. It could be hours."

Kate backed away until she felt the edge of her worktable. "I'll wait in the sitting room."

"In the dark? Without heat?" Devon shook his head. "The temperature is dropping already. This wing will be uncomfortably cold within the hour."

Rain thrashed against the windows, and Kate felt a chill spread across her arms The studio, with its large windows, was already cooling.

"What do you suggest?" she asked warily.

"The main house has a backup generator for essential areas," Devon said. "My private quarters, the kitchen, and some common rooms There's a fireplace in the library that would provide both light and warmth."

Kate hesitated. Entering the main house, Devon's domain, felt like crossing a forbidden threshold. But the thought of spending hours in the increasingly cold, dark studio was equally unappealing.

"I don't have much choice, do I?" she said finally.

"There's always choice, Kate," Devon replied, his voice soft. "I'm offering comfort and safety, not making demands."

Another violent thunderclap shook the windows, making the decision for her. "Fine. Lead the way."

Devon pulled out a flashlight and lit a path through the sitting room to the door connecting to the main house. This door, unlike the one to her bedroom, opened easily. Electronic locks, Kate realized, could be both prison and protection, depending on who held the power.

They moved through darkened corridors, the flashlight beam creating a tunnel of visibility. Kate stayed several paces behind Devon, memorizing their route, noting landmarks and counting turns. The main house was a maze, much larger than she had imagined. They passed closed doors, darkened rooms, and art-lined corridors before Devon stopped before a set of double doors.

"The library," he said, pushing them open.

The room beyond was a bibliophile's dream. Two stories of bookshelves, comfortable reading nooks, and a massive stone fireplace. The room was illuminated by an already burning fire and a few oil lamps. Kate moved toward the fire, drawn by its warmth despite her suspicion.

"Please, make yourself comfortable," Devon said, gesturing to the seating. "Would you like something to drink? Tea, perhaps, or something stronger?"

Kate chose an armchair, positioning herself with the fire between them. "Tea," she said, selecting the option least likely to cloud her judgment.

Devon nodded and moved to a side table where a tea service waited. Kate noted the preparation, the orchestration. Had Devon somehow arranged the power failure? It seemed far-fetched, but the readiness with which he had appeared, the prepared library, the waiting tea service… it all seemed too convenient.

"You think I engineered this situation," Devon said, reading her expression as he handed her a steaming cup. "Created the storm, knocked out the power, all to lure you here."

Kate accepted the tea but didn't drink. "The thought crossed my mind."

Devon smiled slightly. "I'm flattered by your estimation of my powers, but even vampires can't control the weather. This is simply fortunate timing from my perspective, unfortunate from yours."

"And the prepared library? The tea?"

"I maintain several comfortable spaces with backup power and heat for exactly these situations," Devon explained. "As for the tea, I asked for it to be prepared when I realized you would likely join me.

Kate took a cautious sip of her tea. It was prepared exactly the way she liked it with a splash of milk and no sugar, yet another reminder of Devon's detailed surveillance of her habits.

The storm continued to wage its war outside, while inside the fire provided solace. The contrast created an atmosphere of intimate isolation; they might have been the only two people in the world, sheltered together against the elements.

"How long do these power outages typically last?" Kate asked.

"It varies," Devon replied. "A few hours, usually. Sometimes longer if there's significant damage."

"And we're just supposed to sit here until then?"

Devon gestured to the thousands of books. "There are worse places to be stranded. Feel free to explore the collection. Many of these volumes are quite rare."

Kate glanced at the nearest shelf, noting leather-bound tomes. Books had always been a refuge. "You're a collector of books as well as art," she observed.

"I've had a long time to accumulate things that interest me," Devon said. "Books, art, music, experiences… they help pass the centuries."

The casual reference to his immortality sent a chill through Kate. It was easy to forget, in this civilized setting, that she was speaking with a creature who had lived for centuries.

"What was the world like?" she found herself asking. "When you were… human?"

The question seemed to surprise Devon. He studied her for a moment.

"Different," he said finally. "Smaller, in some ways. Harsher in others. I was born in the late 17th century, when Europe was recovering from decades of religious wars. Life was brutish and often short for most people."

"How did you become…" Kate gestured vaguely.

"A vampire?" Devon supplied. "I was turned against my will by a noblewoman who took a fancy to me. I was twenty-six, working as a musician in her household. She kept me as her… companion for nearly fifty years before she was killed in a fire."

The matter-of-fact recounting of his origin story struck Kate as surreal. She was having a fireside chat about vampires with her captor during a thunderstorm, like something from a Gothic novel.

"You said she held you captive, and now you're doing the same to me."

Devon's expression darkened. "The situations are not the same. My maker treated me as a plaything, she was cruel for cruelty's sake. I've never harmed you, Kate. I've provided for your comfort, your artistic needs—"

"While keeping me prisoner," Kate interrupted. "The cage may be gilded, but it's still a cage."

"A temporary necessity," Devon insisted. "Until you understand that I mean you no harm, that I only want—"

"What? What do you want from me?" Kate demanded.

Devon was silent for a long moment. "Understanding," he said finally. "Connection. Someone who sees the world as I do, who transforms pain into beauty as you do with your art."

"You can't force connection," Kate said. "You can't kidnap understanding."

"No," Devon agreed, surprising her. "I can't. I realized that within days of bringing you here. But I couldn't release you either, not after you'd seen what I am. And so we're at an impasse."

The admission hung in the air, accompanied by the crackling of the fire and the rumble of distant thunder. The storm was moving away, but its presence still dominated the night.

As Kate studied Devon across the firelight, a thought occurred to her. For the first time, she saw not just the monster who had abducted her, but a being caught in his own form of captivity, imprisoned by immortality, the need for blood, and centuries of isolation. It didn't excuse his actions, but it offered a potential leverage point.

If Devon truly wanted connection, understanding… perhaps she could appear to offer it. She could play the role he wanted, seem to soften toward him, and accept her situation. It could mean more freedom within the estate and more opportunities to find potential escape routes.

The realization must have shown on her face, because Devon tilted his head slightly, studying her with newfound interest. "What are you thinking?" he asked.

Kate chose her words carefully. "I'm thinking that we're both stuck in this situation, at least for now. And that perhaps… perhaps there's a middle ground between your captivity and my freedom."

"What sort of middle ground?" Devon asked, caution and hope mingling in his voice.

"Less locked doors," Kate suggested. "More trust. A chance to… understand each other better."

Devon's eyes narrowed slightly. "Such a sudden change of heart."

Kate shrugged, trying to appear casual. "The storm changed things. Sitting here, talking like this, it's the first time I've seen you as something other than my jailer." The lie came more easily than she expected, possibly because it contained a grain of truth. "I'm not saying I forgive you for abducting me, but I'm tired of living in constant fear and anger. It's exhausting."

"And what would you want in return for this… understanding?" Devon asked, still wary but clearly intrigued.

"More freedom within the estate," Kate said. "Access to the main house, the grounds. The ability to move about without locked doors and constant supervision."

Devon considered her request. "And if I granted this, what guarantees would I have that you wouldn't try to escape at the first opportunity?"

Kate met his gaze steadily. "None. You'd have to trust me, just as I'd have to trust that more freedom doesn't come with… other expectations."

"By which you mean?"

"Physical expectations," Kate clarified, her cheeks warming despite her resolve to remain clinical. "If I'm to have more freedom in your home, it can't be conditional on… intimacy."

Devon looked genuinely offended. "I would never force myself on you, Kate. Whatever you may think of me, I'm not a rapist."

"Good," Kate said firmly. "Then we understand each other."

Sparks flew up from the fireplace as a log shifted. The storm was over, the night air now quiet and hushed. The air between Kate and Devon, however, vibrated with a new kind of tension. Kate had made her move. Now, it was Devon's turn to respond.

Chapter 6

Two weeks had passed since the thunderstorm that had forced Kate and Devon into their first real conversation. Two weeks of careful performance on Kate's part: Small smiles over shared meals, thoughtful questions about Devon's past, and a gradual relaxation of her rigid boundaries. Two weeks of expanding freedom as Devon, encouraged by her apparent softening, granted her access to more areas of the estate.

Tonight's dinner was being held in the formal dining room rather than the smaller breakfast room where she had taken her previous meals. The space was impressive with a long table that could seat twenty, crystal chandeliers casting warm light over antique furnishings, and floor-to-ceiling windows.

Kate had dressed with particular care, selecting a simple but elegant black dress from the wardrobe Devon had provided. She didn't want to imply romantic interest, but she did want to show that she was taking the dinner seriously. Her hair was loose around her shoulders, and she wore little makeup. Attractive but not seductive, engaged but not eager.

She entered the dining room to find Devon already waiting. He stood near one of the windows, a glass of red substance in hand, and turned at the sound of her entrance. For a moment, he simply looked at her, his expression one of quiet appreciation.

"You look lovely," he said finally.

"Thank you," Kate replied, accepting the compliment with a small smile. "This is quite a room. Do you often dine so formally?"

Devon moved to pull out her chair at one end of the table. Rather than sitting at the opposite end, he had arranged their places at adjacent corners, close enough for conversation without invading personal space.

"Rarely," he admitted, taking his own seat after she was settled. "The formal dining room sees use perhaps three or four times a year, for special occasions."

"And what are we celebrating tonight?" Kate asked, unfolding her napkin and placing it in her lap.

Devon's eyes met hers over the rim of his wineglass. "Progress," he said simply.

A staff member appeared silently to pour wine for Kate and serve the first course, a delicate soup that smelled of herbs and subtle spices. Kate took a careful sip, finding it delicious.

"You're not eating?" she observed, noting that Devon had no plate before him.

"I don't require conventional nourishment," he reminded her gently. "Though I do enjoy wine. The sensory experience remains pleasurable even if the alcohol has no effect."

Kate nodded, taking another spoonful of soup to hide her discomfort. It was these casual reminders of Devon's inhuman nature that helped maintain her resolve. When he spoke of literature or music, when he shared stories of his travels or listened attentively to her thoughts on art, it was easy to forget what he was. But then would come these jarring reminders: He didn't eat, he slept during daylight hours, he drank blood to survive.

"You're thinking about what I am again," Devon said, his perception uncomfortably accurate. "I can see it in your expression, that moment of remembering and recoiling."

Kate considered denying it, then decided honesty might serve her better in this instance. "It's... difficult to wrap my head around sometimes. The person I speak with and the... vampire."

"They're one and the same," Devon said. "My nature doesn't change based on what activity I'm engaged in."

"I know that intellectually," Kate admitted. "But emotionally, it's more complicated."

Devon nodded, seeming to appreciate her candor. "May I ask you something, Kate?"

She tensed slightly but nodded.

"Are you still planning to escape at the first opportunity?"

The question caught her off guard, though perhaps it shouldn't have. Devon was perceptive, cautious, it would be naive to think he hadn't considered the possibility that her softening was strategic rather than genuine.

Kate set down her spoon and considered how best to respond without raising his suspicions.

"I think about freedom every day," she said finally, "I miss my life, my independence, that hasn't changed."

"But?" Devon prompted, sensing there was more.

"But I'm also… adjusting to this reality," Kate continued. "Finding ways to live within it rather than constantly fighting against it. That's not the same as acceptance, but it's… something."

Devon studied her face, searching for deception. Kate met his gaze steadily, allowing him to see what she wanted him to see, a conflicted woman gradually adjusting to her circumstances while still yearning for what she had lost.

"Thank you for your honesty," he said finally.

The first course was cleared away and replaced with the main dish, a perfectly prepared filet with roasted vegetables. Kate ate slowly, using the meal as a buffer for conversation.

"You mentioned you were a musician before you were turned," she said, steering the conversation to safer ground. "What instrument did you play?"

Devon's expression lightened. "Primarily the viola da gamba, though I was proficient with several string instruments of the period. Music was my first artistic love, long before I developed an appreciation for painting or literature."

"And that's why you still play the piano?"

"Yes, though I didn't learn piano until the mid-18th century. It was still a relatively new instrument when I first encountered it."

Kate tried to imagine the span of Devon's existence, centuries of human history experienced firsthand rather than read about in books. Despite herself, she was fascinated.

"What was it like?" she asked. "Watching the world change so dramatically over centuries?"

Devon considered the question, swirling the wine in his glass. "Gradual and sudden, both at once. Day to day, little seems to change. But then you look back over decades or centuries and realize everything is different. I've lived through political and industrial revolutions, seen empires rise and fall, watched as humanity's understanding of the universe expanded exponentially."

"It sounds overwhelming," Kate said.

Devon nodded. "It can be, that's why I value art and music. They remain my constants, an anchor to my former human life. Human experiences become immortalized when they are transcribed to paper or canvas. Your paintings could have been created in any era; the emotions they convey are timeless."

The compliment, specific and thoughtful, warmed Kate, and for a second, she let her guard down.

"Speaking of art," Devon continued, "I have something to show you after dinner, if you're open to it?"

Kate's curiosity was piqued despite her caution. "What is it?"

"A surprise," Devon said, a small smile playing at the corners of his mouth. "But one I think you'll appreciate."

After dinner finished, Devon led Kate through corridors she hadn't yet explored, deeper into the main house. They walked up a grand staircase to the second floor where the hallways were lined with paintings and sculptures that would have been at home in any major museum.

"Your collection is remarkable," Kate observed, pausing to examine a small Degas that hung between two larger landscapes.

"I've had centuries to acquire pieces that speak to me," Devon replied. "Though I've sold or donated many works over the years as well. I believe art should be seen, appreciated, not hoarded away."

"Says the man with a private collection that rivals the Met," Kate teased, the banter coming more naturally than she had expected.

Devon laughed, the sound rich and genuine. "Touché. Though in my defense, I do loan pieces to museums regularly."

They continued down the hallway until Devon stopped before a set of double doors. "Close your eyes," he requested.

Kate hesitated, instinctive wariness warring with curiosity.

"Please," Devon added. "I want this to be a proper surprise."

After a moment's consideration, Kate closed her eyes. She heard the doors open, felt Devon's hand very lightly at her elbow, guiding her forward a few steps.

"Now you can look," he said, his voice close to her ear.

Kate opened her eyes and gasped involuntarily. They stood in a circular room with a domed glass ceiling that revealed the night sky above, stars brilliant against the darkness. But it was the walls that had prompted her reaction. They were covered floor to ceiling with paintings. Her paintings.

Not just the pieces Devon had purchased over the years, but reproductions of works she had sold to other collectors, photographs of installations she had created, even prints of student works she had posted online but never exhibited publicly. It was a comprehensive retrospective of her artistic journey, arranged chronologically around the circular space.

"How did you…" Kate began, moving toward the nearest wall where her earliest works hung.

"As I said, I've been following your career for three years," Devon explained, remaining by the door to give her space to explore. "When I first saw your work, I was… moved in a way I hadn't experienced in decades."

Kate moved slowly around the room, taking in the visual record of her artistic evolution. It was strange and somewhat unsettling to see her life's work assembled this way, curated by someone else's hand. But it was also oddly touching, the care with which the pieces had been arranged, the attention to detail.

She finally turned to face Devon. "This is either the most flattering thing anyone has ever done for me, or the most stalkerish."

Devon dipped his head as a self-deprecating smile spread over his face. "Perhaps a bit of both. I wanted to show you that my interest in your work is genuine. That it wasn't a whim that brought me to your exhibition in Budapest."

Kate continued her circuit of the room, stopping before a reproduction of

"Crimson Storm," the painting Devon had commented on at the gallery, the one that had sparked their first real conversation.

"You said this reminded you of your own rage," she said, studying the violent slashes of red and black.

Devon moved to stand beside her, his eyes on the painting rather than on her. "Yes. The contained violence of it, the beauty wrought from pain, resonated deeply. Your work reveals a soul that understands darkness but chooses to create, rather than destroy. Someone who transforms pain into beauty rather than bitterness. That's… rare."

Kate turned to look at him, finding his face more open, more vulnerable than she had seen it before. In that moment, she could almost forget what he was, what he had done. Almost.

"This room is remarkable," she said, sweeping her hand around the gallery. "Thank you for showing it to me."

"It's yours," Devon replied. "To visit whenever you wish. I've added your biometric data to the security system, these doors will open only for you and me."

The gesture was significant, not just the access to a new space, but the privacy it offered. A room that was hers alone, apart from Devon himself.

"Thank you," Kate said again, meaning it this time.

They stood in silence for a moment, surrounded by the visual record of Kate's artistic journey. The space between them seemed charged with unspoken thoughts, with the complexity of their situation. Captor and captive, artist and patron, two damaged souls recognizing something in each other despite the circumstances that had brought them together.

"It's getting late," Devon said finally. "I should escort you back to your suite."

Kate nodded, reluctant to leave the gallery but aware of the dangerous territory their conversation was approaching. As they walked back through the corridors, she found herself more confused than she had been at the start of the evening. The calculated performance she had planned had become muddied by genuine reactions.

She had been moved by the gallery, touched by Devon's evident appreciation of her work. She had enjoyed their conversation about art and history, had been fascinated by his perspectives on centuries of human experience. None of that had been feigned, and that realization disturbed her deeply.

At the door to her suite, Devon paused. "Thank you for joining me tonight, Kate."

"Thank you for dinner," she replied automatically. "And for showing me the gallery."

Devon studied her face for a moment, as if memorizing its features. Then, slowly enough that she could have stepped away had she chosen to, he reached out to tuck a strand of hair behind her ear. His fingers were cool against her skin, the touch feather-light and gone almost instantly.

"Good night," he said softly, turning to leave before she could respond.

Kate closed the door behind her and leaned against it, heart racing, skin still tingling where his fingers had brushed her ear. The touch had been so brief, so innocent compared to the liberties he could have taken. Yet it had affected her more than she cared to admit.

"It's just Stockholm Syndrome," she whispered to herself, pushing away from the door and moving toward her bedroom. "Textbook captor-captive psychology. It doesn't mean anything."

But as she prepared for bed, Kate couldn't shake the memory of Devon's expression as he showed her the gallery, the genuine vulnerability, the hope for understanding. She also couldn't deny the flutter she had felt in her belly when he touched her hair.

Her plan to manipulate Devon into granting her more freedom was working perfectly. The problem, Kate realized with growing dismay, was that the lines between performance and reality were beginning to blur, not just for Devon, but for herself as well.

Drifting towards sleep, Kate reminded herself firmly of her ultimate goal: Escape. She couldn't afford to lose sight of that and allow herself to be seduced by Devon's charm or his apparent understanding of her art.

No matter how the lines blurred, she had to remember the truth: She was a prisoner, and he was her captor. Everything else was illusion, manipulation, or the psychological response of a captive seeking to survive.

Wasn't it?

Chapter 7

Kate had been watching the deliveries for three weeks now. The white van came every Monday and Thursday morning at 9:15 AM. The same young woman always drove, clipboard in hand, overseeing the unloading of supplies with brisk efficiency.

From her hidden vantage point behind a stand of ornamental shrubs, Kate had observed the routine multiple times, noting every detail. The delivery took roughly twenty minutes. The staff who received the goods were always the same three people. The estate's cook, a middle-aged man who appeared to be the head of household staff, and a younger assistant who helped with the heavy lifting. The delivery woman would joke with them, sign forms, and occasionally accept a cup of coffee before departing.

Most importantly, Kate had observed that the delivery woman was never searched, nor was the van inspected upon exit. The security at the service entrance seemed to operate on recognition and routine rather than strict protocols.

Today, Kate decided to make contact. After weeks of careful performance with Devon, she had earned enough trust to move freely around the estate grounds during daylight hours. The staff had been instructed not to interfere with her activities, though she suspected they kept tabs on her and reported her movements to Devon.

She wore casual clothes that wouldn't draw attention and had her hair tied up. She wanted to appear as non-threatening and ordinary as possible. In her pocket was a small sketch she had made, a pretext for the conversation she planned to initiate.

As the delivery van pulled up to the service entrance, Kate began walking purposefully along the path that would take her past the loading area. She timed her approach to coincide with the moment when the delivery woman would be checking items off her clipboard, after the initial unloading but before departure.

Kate's heart hammered in her chest as she drew closer. This was risky, if the staff reported this interaction to Devon, he might become suspicious. But it was a calculated risk, one she needed to take if her escape plan was to have any chance of success. The delivery woman was leaning against the van, sipping from a paper cup of coffee and checking her list when Kate approached. She glanced up, mild surprise registering on her face at seeing someone new.

"Good morning," Kate said, offering a friendly smile.

"Morning," the young woman replied, her tone cautious but not unfriendly. She looked about twenty-five with brown hair pulled back in a ponytail and intelligent eyes that assessed Kate quickly.

"I'm Kate," she said, extending her hand. "I'm staying at the estate for a while."

The delivery woman hesitated only briefly before shaking Kate's hand. "Mira," she replied. "I do the deliveries for Harvest Fresh."

"I've noticed," Kate said, then quickly added, "I take walks in the morning. I've seen the van a few times."

Mira nodded, her expression neutral, but her eyes curious. Guests at the Karlov estate were rare, and those who approached delivery staff even rarer.

"I'm an artist," Kate continued, pulling the small sketch from her pocket. "I've been drawing the estate grounds. I thought this spot had an interesting perspective, but I'm not sure I captured it right. Would you mind taking a look? Sometimes a fresh eye helps."

It was a transparent excuse, but it served its purpose. Mira set down her clipboard and accepted the sketch, a quick but skillful rendering of the service entrance area, with the mountains visible in the background.

"This is really good," Mira said, genuine appreciation in her voice. "You've got the light just right. The way it hits the stone wall here."

"Thanks," Kate said, moving to stand beside Mira as if to see the sketch from her perspective. Lowering her voice, she added, "I need help."

Mira's body tensed slightly, but her expression remained neutral. She continued to look at the sketch as if they were still discussing art.

"What kind of help?" she asked quietly, her eyes flicking briefly to the estate staff who were still busy organizing the delivered goods.

"I'm not a guest here," Kate whispered. "I'm being held against my will."

Mira's eyes widened slightly, but she maintained her composure. "By Mr Karlov?"

Kate nodded minutely. "I need to get a message out. Or better yet, find a way out myself."

Mira was silent for a moment, her eyes still on the sketch. "Mr Karlov has been good to my family," she said finally. "He helped my mother when she was sick, paid for treatments the insurance wouldn't cover. He's always been fair with our business."

Kate's heart sank. Of course Devon would have cultivated loyalty in the local community. It was both smart and strategic, and now it was an obstacle.

"I understand," Kate said, preparing to retreat before she made things worse.

"But," Mira continued, her voice barely audible, "I've heard stories about this place. About Mr Karlov's… unusual habits."

Hope flickered in Kate's chest. "What have you heard?"

Mira glanced at the staff again, then handed the sketch back to Kate. In a normal voice, she said, "It's really good. You've got talent."

Then, more quietly: "I deliver again on Thursday. Same time. Draw another sketch with any message you want to send out. I can't promise anything, but I'll look at it."

"Thank you," Kate breathed, taking back the sketch.

Mira nodded almost imperceptibly, then picked up her clipboard. "I should finish up here. Nice meeting you, Kate."

"You too, Mira," Kate replied, tucking the sketch back into her pocket.

As she walked away, Kate felt a mixture of hope and anxiety. She had made contact, found someone who might be willing to help, or at least to listen.

But she had also taken a huge risk. If Mira mentioned this interaction to anyone, if the staff reported it to Devon…

Kate pushed the worry aside. She couldn't afford to let fear paralyze her. She had three days to prepare her next move, to decide what message to include with her next sketch. Three days to continue her performance with Devon while secretly preparing her escape.

Kate rounded the corner of the main house and almost ran into a man coming from the other direction. Her heart missed a beat as she recognized Devon's assistant, Marcus. He was a silent, efficient man who served as Devon's daytime proxy when necessary.

"Ms Morgan," Marcus said, his tone formal. "Mr Karlov requests your presence in the music room this evening at eight. He mentioned something about a surprise."

"Thank you, Marcus," Kate replied, keeping her voice steady despite her racing pulse. "Please tell him I'll be there."

Marcus nodded and continued on his way, giving no indication that he found her presence near the service entrance suspicious. Kate released a breath she hadn't realized she was holding.

Her first contact with Mira had gone undetected, it seemed. Now she just needed to maintain her performance with Devon while carefully nurturing this potential avenue of escape.

The dual track of her existence, the growing complexity of her relationship with Devon alongside her determined pursuit of freedom, was becoming complicated and muddied.

But Kate was committed to both paths, even as they seemed to diverge further with each passing day.

* * *

Kate didn't know what to expect that evening as she stepped into the music room. Dozens of candles illuminated the space in a warm glow. Devon's piano stood in the center, but it was the easel set up next to it that caught Kate's eye. A bare canvas was propped on it with paints and brushes neatly arranged nearby.

Devon stood by the piano, dressed more casually than usual in dark trousers and a white that emphasized his broad shoulders. He turned as she entered, a smile lighting his features.

"Kate," he said, her name a warm greeting on his lips. "Thank you for coming."

"Marcus said you had a surprise," Kate replied, moving further into the room but maintaining a careful distance.

Devon gestured to the easel and piano. "I thought we might try something… collaborative. I play, you paint, responding to the music, creating something together."

The idea was unexpectedly appealing. Kate had experimented with painting to music before, but never with a live musician, never with someone playing specifically for her.

"What would you play?" she asked, approaching the easel to examine the supplies. Everything was high quality, as always.

"Whatever inspires you," Devon replied. "Classical, contemporary, improvisation, the choice is yours."

Kate ran her fingers over the brushes, considering. This wasn't part of her plan, spending an evening creating art with Devon rather than using the time to prepare for her next contact with Mira. But the opportunity to paint freely, lose herself in creation while surrounded by music… it was tempting.

"Chopin," she said finally, remembering their dance at the gallery. "The piece we danced to."

Devon's smile deepened, pleasure evident in his eyes. "Aeolian Harp. An excellent choice."

He moved to the piano bench and sat, flexing his fingers before positioning them over the keys. "Whenever you're ready," he said, waiting for her cue.

Kate picked up a brush, dipped it in a rich blue, and nodded. Devon began to play, the familiar notes filling the room with their emotional resonance. Kate closed her eyes briefly, letting the music wash over her, then began to paint.

For the next hour, they existed in a strange harmony, Devon playing with the skill of centuries of practice, Kate responding to the music with bold strokes of color and form. The canvas gradually filled with a visual interpretation of the concerto, swirling blues and purples for the melancholic passages, fiery reds and oranges for the passionate crescendos.

Kate lost herself in the process, forgetting momentarily about escape plans and delivery women, about captivity and freedom. There was only the music, the canvas, and the peculiar connection that formed between artist and musician as they created together.

When Devon reached the final movement of the concerto, Kate found herself painting with increasing intensity, her brushstrokes becoming more urgent and emotional.

When the final notes faded, Kate stepped back from the canvas, breathing heavily as if she had been running. The painting before her was unlike anything she had created before, more raw and immediate.

Devon rose from the piano bench and moved to stand beside her, studying the canvas with evident appreciation. "It's extraordinary," he said softly.

Kate was still caught in the creative trance, her defenses lowered by the intensity of the experience. "It was the music," she said. "Your playing, it was beautiful."

Devon turned to look at her, something vulnerable and hopeful in his expression. "We created something together," he said. "Something neither of us could have made alone."

The intimacy of the moment, the shared creative experience, the way Devon was looking at her, it all combined to create a dangerous emotional undercurrent. Kate felt herself being pulled toward him, not physically but emotionally, the barriers she had carefully maintained beginning to crumble.

"I should go," she said abruptly, setting down her brush. "It's getting late."

Devon's expression shifted, confusion and disappointment replacing the openness of a moment before. "Kate? What's wrong?"

"Nothing," she said too quickly. "I'm just tired. It's been a long day."

Devon wasn't fooled. He studied her face, easily picking up the sudden shift in her demeanor. "You're afraid," he said, his voice gentle but certain. "Not of me, I think, but of this—" he gestured between them and the painting

"—of what we just shared."

"I'm not afraid," Kate insisted, but the tremor in her voice betrayed her.

"You are," Devon countered. "Because for a moment, you forgot to perform. You were simply yourself, creating with me, enjoying the experience. And that terrifies you."

Kate felt exposed, as if Devon had peered directly into her mind and seen the conflict there, the genuine enjoyment of their artistic collaboration warring with her determination to maintain emotional distance.

"You don't know what I'm thinking," she said, her voice hardening as she tried to rebuild her walls.

"Don't I?" Devon moved closer, not touching her but entering her personal space. "I've watched you for weeks now, Kate. I've seen the careful performance, the measured smiles, the calculated questions, the strategic softening. And I've also seen the rare moments of genuine response, like tonight when you lost yourself in the painting."

Kate took a step back, alarmed by his perception and by her own slip. "I don't know what you're talking about."

"I think you do," Devon said, his voice still gentle but now tinged with something harder. "I think you've been playing a role, hoping to gain my trust, to earn more freedom. Perhaps even planning an escape."

Kate's heart raced, fear coursing through her. Had he seen her with Mira? Had the staff reported their interaction?

"That's ridiculous," she said, trying to sound indignant rather than terrified. "I've been trying to make the best of an impossible situation. To find some way to live with what you've done to me."

Devon was silent for a long moment, his eyes never leaving her face. "I want to believe you," he said finally. "I want to believe that what we just shared was real, that the connection I felt wasn't one-sided or manufactured."

The vulnerability in his admission caught Kate off guard. Despite everything, his age, his power, his inhuman nature, Devon was capable of being hurt by her deception. The realization was uncomfortable, complicating her neat categorization of him as simply her captor, her enemy.

"I don't know what you want from me," Kate said, her voice softer now, confusion evident in her tone.

"Honesty," Devon replied simply. "Even if it's painful. Even if it's that you're planning to leave the moment an opportunity presents itself."

Kate looked away, unable to meet his gaze. The moment stretched between them, taut with unspoken truths and complicated emotions.

"I think about escape every day," she admitted finally, deciding that a version of honesty might salvage the situation. "How could I not? You took me from my life, my home, my freedom. Of course I want those things back."

Devon nodded, accepting this without visible reaction. "And the rest? The moments like tonight, when you seem to… connect with me?"

Kate hesitated, caught between strategic deception and uncomfortable truth. "They're… confusing," she said at last, offering a genuine admission. "I don't want to feel anything for you except anger. But sometimes…"

She trailed off, unwilling to complete the thought even to herself.

Devon stepped back, giving her space. "Thank you for your honesty," he said, his voice carefully controlled. "It's late, as you said. I'll escort you back to your suite."

The walk through the corridors was silent, the easy rapport they had shared during their creative collaboration replaced by tension and unspoken thoughts. At her door, Devon paused.

"Despite what you may believe, Kate, I do value truth between us, even when it's something I don't want to hear."

He turned to leave, his footsteps echoing down the corridor. Inside her room, Kate leaned against the closed door, her heart pounding away, her breath shaky. Devon's words had struck a nerve. They had revealed an uncomfortable truth she had been trying to ignore. The lines were blurring and it terrified her.

Getting into bed, she tried to cling to her determination to escape, but the memory of Devon's vulnerable expression, the shared creative energy, and the unsettling flutter of something that resembled attraction made it difficult.

"It's all just an act," she whispered to herself, a desperate mantra. "It doesn't mean anything."

Deep down in her core, she knew that she was lying to herself. A connection was forming, one that defied logic and threatened to unravel her carefully constructed defenses.

The game had changed, and Kate was no longer sure who was playing whom.

Chapter 8

By the time Thursday morning arrived Kate was filled with more determination and focus than she had felt in weeks. The three days following her confrontation with Devon had been tense, but not disastrous. He hadn't taken away her freedoms or confined her to her suite as she had feared. Instead, he maintained a careful distance. Their interactions were polite, but lacked the warmth that had begun to develop before her performance slipped.

In many ways the distance was a relief, it gave Kate space to think and prepare for her next meeting with Mira. In other ways, it was unsettling. She found herself missing their conversations, their shared appreciation of art and music. The painting they had created together now hung in her studio, a constant reminder of the genuine connection they had briefly shared.

But today wasn't about Devon or complicated feelings. Today was about escape, about freedom, about reclaiming her life. Kate had prepared carefully. In her pocket was a new sketch of the mountains visible from the estate gardens. On the back, written in small, neat letters, was her message to Mira:

I need to escape. You and I look alike. If you help me take your place in the delivery van, I can get away. I can pay you, there's jewelry in my room worth thousands. Please help me. Monday?

It was direct, but Kate couldn't afford misunderstanding at this point. Her time at the estate had already stretched far longer than she had ever anticipated, and with each passing day, the risk of becoming too comfortable, too accepting of her gilded cage, grew greater.

At precisely 9:10 AM, Kate positioned herself along the path that would take her past the service entrance. She had timed her morning walks to coincide with deliveries over the past week, establishing a pattern that wouldn't seem suspicious to any watching staff. Today would appear no different, just another morning stroll that happened to pass the delivery area.

The white van pulled up right on schedule. Kate waited until the unloading was underway before approaching, her heart hammering in her chest but her exterior calm and casual.

Mira was checking items off her clipboard when she spotted Kate. A flicker of recognition crossed her features, followed by a carefully neutral expression.

"Good morning," Kate called, her tone friendly but not overly familiar.

"Morning," Mira replied, her eyes darting briefly to the estate staff before returning to Kate.

"Another walk?"

"Yes, the gardens are beautiful this time of day," Kate said, the casual conversation a cover for her approach. "I've been working on another sketch, actually. Would you mind taking a look? I value your opinion."

It was the same pretext as before, but it served its purpose. Mira set down her clipboard and stepped slightly away from the loading area, creating a small bubble of privacy.

"Sure, I'd be happy to," she said, accepting the folded paper Kate offered. Mira studied the sketch for a moment, then carefully turned it over, her expression unchanging as she read the message on the back. Her eyes flicked up to meet Kate's, a silent communication passing between them.

"The perspective is good," Mira said aloud, for the benefit of anyone who might be watching. "You've really captured the mountains well." Then, her voice dropping to a whisper: "Monday is too soon. Next Thursday. I need time to prepare."

Kate nodded as she pretended to look over the sketch with Mira. "Thank you," she said at normal volume. "I appreciate the feedback. I'm still learning to capture landscapes properly."

Lowering her voice, she added, "Thursday it is."

Mira handed the sketch back, her expression still carefully neutral. "Keep practicing. You're getting better with each attempt." In a whisper: "Bring as much jewelry as you can carry. I'm risking a lot."

Kate nodded slightly, accepting both the artistic "advice" and the terms. "I will. Thanks again for looking."

Mira returned to her clipboard, the interaction concluding as naturally as it had begun. "See you around," she said, a loaded statement given their whispered agreement.

"Definitely," Kate replied, tucking the sketch back into her pocket and continuing her walk as if nothing significant had transpired.

As she rounded the corner of the main house, Kate allowed herself a small smile of triumph. The plan was in motion. One week from today, she would be free. All she needed to do was maintain her performance with Devon for seven more days, gather the promised payment for Mira, and prepare for the moment when she would walk out the service gate in a delivery uniform, leaving her gilded cage behind.

The thought should have filled her with absolute joy, but it came with a complicated undercurrent of emotion she wasn't ready to examine too closely.

* * *

Kate worked away in her studio that evening on a new canvas. The painting was different from her usual style, more controlled and less explosive. Perhaps it reflected her current state of mind: Focused, strategic, compartmentalizing the complicated feelings that threatened to upturn her plans.

She was so absorbed in her work that she didn't hear the studio door open. It was only when a shadow fell across her canvas that she realized she was no longer alone. Devon stood a few feet away, watching her paint with an expression of quiet appreciation. He was dressed formally in a tailored suit, his dark hair combed back from his forehead.

"I didn't mean to startle you," he said, noting her surprise. "I knocked, but you were deep in concentration."

Kate set down her brush and wiped her hands on a cloth. "That's alright," she said, keeping her tone carefully neutral. "I lose track of time when I'm painting."

Devon nodded, understanding in his eyes. "I'm the same way with music. Hours pass like minutes when I'm at the piano." The reference to their shared creative experience hung in the air between them, neither acknowledging it directly but both aware of its significance.

"You look nice," Kate observed, gesturing to his formal attire. "Special occasion?"

"Actually, yes," Devon replied. "There's a concert in Budapest this evening, a pianist I've admired for decades is performing Chopin. I have a private box at the concert hall."

Kate nodded, waiting for him to continue, sensing there was more to this visit than sharing his evening plans.

"I was hoping you might accompany me," Devon said, a hint of uncertainty in his voice that seemed at odds with his usual confidence. The invitation caught Kate off guard. In all her weeks at the estate, Devon had never suggested leaving the grounds together.

"You want me to go to Budapest with you?" she asked, making sure she understood correctly.

"Yes," Devon confirmed. "The concert begins at eight. We would return to the estate afterward, of course."

The "of course" was a reminder of her status, this wasn't freedom, just a longer leash. Still, the opportunity to leave the estate, to be in a public place with potential witnesses or even opportunities to signal for help, was too valuable to dismiss. But there was another consideration, one Kate was reluctant to acknowledge even to herself. The prospect of spending an evening with Devon, sharing an experience they would both genuinely appreciate, held an appeal that had nothing to do with escape plans or strategic performance.

"I'd like that," she said, surprising herself with the sincerity in her voice.

"Thank you for the invitation."

Devon's expression lightened, pleasure evident in his eyes. "Excellent. We should leave in about an hour, if that gives you enough time to prepare?" Kate glanced down at her paint-spattered clothes and smiled ruefully. "I'll need every minute of it."

"I'll meet you in the front hall at seven, then," Devon said, turning to leave. As he reached the door, he paused and looked back at her. "The blue dress in your wardrobe would be appropriate for the venue, if you're wondering what to wear."

With that, he was gone, leaving Kate to process both the invitation and her complicated response to it.

***

Kate walked down the main staircase an hour later, dressed in the blue gown Devon had suggested. The dress was elegant, deep sapphire silk, cut to flatter without being overtly seductive. She had styled her hair in a simple updo and applied makeup with a light hand, aiming for sophistication rather than glamour.

Devon was waiting at the foot of the stairs, his back to her as he checked his watch. When he turned and saw her, his expression transformed. Surprise, appreciation, and something warmer flickering across his features before he composed himself.

"You look stunning," he said simply.

"Thank you," Kate replied, feeling an unexpected flutter of pleasure at his admiration. "The dress is beautiful."

"The dress is merely fabric," Devon said, offering his arm as she reached the bottom of the stairs. "You're what makes it beautiful."

The compliment was delivered with such sincerity that Kate found herself momentarily speechless. She placed her hand on his offered arm, the contact sending a small shiver through her despite her resolve to remain emotionally detached.

Outside, a sleek black car waited, a driver holding the door open as they approached. Devon helped Kate into the backseat before sliding in beside her, maintaining a respectful distance but close enough that she could detect the subtle scent of his cologne, something woodsy and complex, like the man himself.

As the car pulled away from the estate, Kate felt a surge of conflicting emotions. This was the first time she had left the grounds since Devon took her. She should be using this excursion to her advantage, look for opportunities to escape. Instead, she found herself looking forward to the concert.

"Have you heard this pianist perform before?" she asked, breaking the silence that had settled between them.

"Twice," Devon replied. "Once in Vienna in the 1980s, and again in New York about a decade ago. His interpretation of Chopin is unparalleled, he captures the emotional complexity beneath the technical brilliance."

"You've been following his career for that long?"

Devon smiled slightly. "One advantage of my condition, I can track an artist's entire career, from promising newcomer to established master. I've done the same with painters, writers, musicians… watching their style evolve over decades is a unique privilege."

The reminder of Devon's immortality sent a familiar chill through Kate. It was easy to forget, sitting beside him in the car, that he had lived for centuries, that he would continue to exist long after her own life had ended. The thought was both fascinating and disturbing.

"What's it like?" she asked impulsively. "Watching the world change around you while you remain the same?"

Devon considered the question, his expression thoughtful. "Isolating," he said finally. "Humans form connections knowing they have limited time together. When time becomes essentially unlimited for one party, it changes the nature of every relationship. People age, die, are forgotten by everyone except me."

The loneliness implicit in his answer struck Kate unexpectedly. She had never considered immortality from that perspective, as a condition that separated one from humanity rather than elevating above it.

"Is that why you took me?" she asked, the question emerging before she could reconsider it. "Because you were lonely?"

Devon turned to look at her directly, his eyes reflecting the passing streetlights. "Partly," he admitted. "But I was drawn specifically to you, your art. I recognized something in you that I recognize in myself."

"That doesn't justify abduction," Kate said, but the words lacked their usual heat.

"No," Devon agreed. "It doesn't. I've had centuries to develop wisdom in many areas, but in this, I acted foolishly, impulsively. I saw something precious and tried to possess it, like the art collector I've been for so long."

Kate hadn't expected him to admit his wrongdoing. Before she could respond, the car slowed, turning into the circular drive before the concert hall.

"We've arrived," Devon said, the moment of vulnerability passing as he prepared to exit the vehicle. "Shall we?"

The concert hall was magnificent, a testament to Budapest's imperial past. Devon's private box offered an excellent view of the stage while providing a bit of seclusion from the general audience. Kate was acutely aware of the other patrons glancing their way as they took their seats, curious about the striking couple in the exclusive box.

"People are staring," she murmured to Devon.

"They're looking at you," he replied. "You outshine everyone else in the room."

Before Kate could respond, the house lights dimmed and the pianist walked onto the stage to enthusiastic applause. Over the next hour Kate found herself completely absorbed in the music, now and then glancing over at Devon to find him equally captivated.

The complexities of their situation seemed to fade away in the shared moment. They were simply two people appreciating beauty together, connected by the music. At intermission, Devon handed a flute of champagne to Kate, a small smile playing on his lips.

"Your thoughts?" he asked, genuinely interested in her opinion.

Kate suddenly felt bashful. "I don't pretend to be an expert in classical music, but I can feel the emotion in the notes as he plays; it's beautiful."

Devon nodded, pleased by her observation. "Exactly. Chopin composed emotions, not just music. You know more about classical music than you think."

They discussed the performance as they sipped their champagne, the conversation flowing easily between them. Kate was surprised by how natural it felt, how much she was enjoying herself despite the circumstances that had brought her here.

They returned to their seats as the second half of the concert began. The pianist launched into Chopin's Ballade No. 1 in G minor, an emotionally complex piece. As music rose into a crescendo, Kate felt Devon's hand move to rest beside hers on the armrest they shared. She remained still, aware of the proximity. Then, in a decision she would later struggle to explain even to herself, she shifted her hand slightly until her fingers brushed against his.

Devon remained perfectly still, as if afraid any movement might break the slight contact. Then, slowly, he turned his hand palm up, an invitation rather than a demand. Kate hesitated, the rational part of her mind screaming warnings about boundaries and manipulation. But another part, the part that had connected with Devon through art and music and conversation, urged her to accept the small intimacy.

As the music reached a particularly moving passage, Kate placed her hand in his. Devon's fingers closed gently around hers, the contact sending a jolt through her. It was a silent acknowledgment of the growing, undeniable pull between them.

It was a small gesture, but in the grand, ornate concert hall, surrounded by strangers, it felt like a secret, an intimacy that transcended their complicated reality. The music swelled, carrying them both on its emotional tide, and for a fleeting moment, Kate forgot everything but the warmth of Devon's hand in hers, and the dangerous, exhilarating thrill of a connection she was no longer sure she wanted to escape.

They remained that way for the rest of the concert, hands joined in the darkened box while Chopin's music swirled around them. It was a small gesture, innocent compared to what could have been, but it represented a crossing of physical boundaries that Kate had carefully maintained until now.

When the concert ended and the house lights came up, they separated naturally, applauding the performer with the rest of the audience. But something had shifted between them, a new awareness that lingered as they made their way out of the concert hall and back to the waiting car.

The drive back to the estate was quieter than the journey into the city, both of them processing the evening's events. As they passed through the gates and approached the main house, Kate found herself reluctant for the night to end, a feeling that both confused and alarmed her.

Devon escorted her to the door of her suite, maintaining a respectful distance as they walked through the corridors. At her door, he paused.

"Thank you for accompanying me tonight," he said, his voice soft in the quiet hallway. "Sharing the experience made it more meaningful."

"Thank you for inviting me," Kate replied with a small smile, meaning it. "It was a beautiful performance."

They stood facing each other, the air between them charged with unspoken thoughts and possibilities. Devon took a small step closer, his eyes searching hers for permission or rejection. Kate knew she should step back, maintain the boundaries that her escape plan required. Instead, she remained still, her heart racing as Devon reached up to brush a strand of hair from her face, his fingers lingering against her cheek.

"Kate," he said, her name almost a question on his lips.

She should pull away. She should say goodnight and close the door between them. She should remember that in one week, she would be gone from this place, from him. Instead, Kate found herself leaning slightly into his touch, her eyes closing briefly at the contact. Devon's hand cupped her cheek gently, his thumb tracing the line of her cheekbone with exquisite care. Then, moving with deliberate slowness, giving her every opportunity to withdraw, he leaned down and pressed his lips to hers.

The kiss was gentle, questioning rather than demanding, a whisper of contact that nevertheless sent electricity coursing through Kate's body. For a moment that seemed both eternal and fleeting, she allowed herself to respond, her lips softening under his, her hand rising to rest against his chest. Then reality reasserted itself, and Kate pulled back, her eyes wide with confusion and something like fear, not of Devon, but of her own response to him.

"I should go inside," she said, her voice unsteady. "It's late."

Devon stepped back immediately, respecting her withdrawal. "Of course," he said, though his eyes reflected a mixture of hope and uncertainty. "Good night, Kate."

"Good night," she replied, slipping through her door and closing it between them.

Inside her suite, Kate leaned against the door, her fingers rising to touch her lips where the sensation of Devon's kiss still lingered. What had she done? What was she doing? In one week, she would be implementing her escape plan, leaving the estate and Devon behind forever. And yet tonight she had allowed—no, participated in—a level of intimacy that complicated everything.

Kate moved to her bedroom, the blue dress suddenly feeling like a costume, a symbol of the evening's departure from her carefully maintained performance. As she changed into her nightclothes, her mind raced with conflicting thoughts and emotions.

The kiss had been, she couldn't even find the right word. Pleasant seemed inadequate, disturbing too negative. It had been affecting, that much she could admit. Devon's gentleness, his restraint, the way he had given her every opportunity to pull away, it all contradicted the image of the controlling captor she needed to maintain in her mind.

But one kiss, one moment of weakness, didn't change the fundamental reality: She was a prisoner, and he was her jailer, regardless of how gentle the confinement. As Kate slipped into bed, she made a silent vow to herself. She would not allow tonight's lapse to derail her plans. In one week, she would leave with Mira's delivery van. She would reclaim her freedom, her life, her autonomy.

And if a small part of her whispered that she might be leaving something precious behind, she pushed it aside. Freedom was worth any price, even the loss of a connection she hadn't sought but couldn't entirely deny.

* * *

Later in the night, Kate woke to unusual sounds in the main house. Raised voices, hurried footsteps in the corridor outside her suite, a general sense of disruption to the estate's usual calm. Curious and slightly alarmed, she dressed quickly and ventured out to investigate.

Staff members moved through the main hall with urgent purpose, carrying supplies and speaking in hushed voices. Marcus stood in the center of the activity, issuing instructions with uncharacteristic emotion in his typically impassive face.

"What's happening?" Kate asked, approaching a staff member she recognized from the kitchen.

The woman glanced at her, hesitation evident in her expression before she replied. "It's Mr Karlov. He's unwell."

Before Kate could ask for more details, Marcus spotted her and moved to intercept, his features composed into their usual mask of professional detachment, though strain showed around his eyes.

"Ms Morgan," he said formally. "Please return to your suite. The household is dealing with a private matter."

"Devon is sick?" Kate pressed, unwilling to be dismissed so easily. "What's wrong with him?"

Marcus hesitated, unsure whether to share the details. "Mr Karlov is experiencing a… medical situation. It's being handled."

"What kind of medical situation?" Kate insisted. "Is it serious?"

Something in her tone, genuine concern rather than mere curiosity, seemed to sway Marcus. His rigid posture softened slightly. "It's a condition that affects his kind sometimes," he said, lowering his voice. "A reaction to… impurities in the blood supply. Mr Karlov received a contaminated feeding yesterday."

The casual reference to "their kind" and "blood supply" sent a chill through Kate, a stark reminder of Devon's inhuman nature. Yet her concern didn't diminish.

"Is he going to be alright?" she asked.

"With proper care, yes," Marcus replied. "The blood donor had undiagnosed leukemia, blood cancer. We screen for many things, but this particular strain was in its very early stages, undetectable by tests. By the time symptoms would have appeared in the human, the cancer cells had already corrupted the blood supply. Cancer cells are toxic to vampires in ways that healthy human blood is not. The next twenty-four hours will be difficult. He's in considerable pain and experiencing other symptoms that are best managed in isolation."

Kate processed this information, trying to imagine what a vampire's illness might entail. "Can I see him?" she asked, surprising both Marcus and herself with the request.

Marcus's eyebrows rose slightly. "That would be unwise. In this condition, Mr Karlov's control over certain… instincts may be compromised. It could be dangerous for you."

"He wouldn't hurt me," Kate said with a certainty that came from somewhere deep and unexamined.

"Not intentionally, no," Marcus conceded. "But in his current state, intentions and actions may not align perfectly."

Kate considered this, weighing the risk against her unexpected but undeniable desire to help. "What does he need? There must be something I can do."

Marcus studied her face, seeming to reassess his understanding of her relationship with Devon. "The contamination must be purged from his system," he explained carefully. "Fresh, pure blood would accelerate the process significantly. We've sent for supplies, but the usual source is… experiencing difficulties. It may be hours before we can get what's needed."

The implication was clear, though Marcus was too diplomatic to state it directly. Devon needed blood, human blood, and the usual supply chain was disrupted. Kate felt a moment of visceral revulsion at the thought, followed by a complex wave of other emotions. Devon was suffering, perhaps seriously ill, because of something as mundane as a contaminated food supply. And she had the power to help him, ease his pain, and potentially save him prolonged suffering.

The rational part of her mind immediately objected. This was her captor, the man who had abducted her, who kept her prisoner despite his gentle treatment and apparent affection. Why should she help him? In fact, wouldn't this be the perfect opportunity for her to slip away and escape, without waiting for Mira and the delivery van? But another part of her, the part that had responded to his kiss last night, that had connected with him through art and music, couldn't dismiss his suffering so easily.

"I want to see him," Kate said again, her voice firmer now. "I want to help."

Marcus was genuinely surprised. "Ms Morgan, while I appreciate your concern, Mr Karlov would never ask this of you. He's been very clear about certain boundaries regarding your stay here."

"He's not asking," Kate pointed out. "I'm offering."

A tense silence stretched between them, Marcus clearly struggling with the decision. Finally, he nodded once, curtly. "I will inform him of your offer," he said. "The choice must be his. Please wait in your suite, and I will bring you his response."

Kate returned to her rooms, her mind racing with the implications of what she had just proposed. Was she really considering allowing Devon to feed from her? The very thought sent a shiver through her body, it was part fear, part something else she wasn't ready to name.

And what about her escape plan? Mira was expecting her in five days. The jewelry was hidden in her studio, ready for the exchange. Everything was in place for her to get away. Helping Devon now, forming another connection, another bond, would only make leaving more difficult.

Yet as she paced her sitting room, waiting for Marcus's return, Kate couldn't shake the image of Devon in pain, suffering alone in his quarters. Whatever he had done, whatever he was, she couldn't simply ignore his need when she had the power to help.

An hour passed before a knock at her door announced Marcus's return. His expression was grave as he delivered Devon's response. "Mr Karlov appreciates your concern and your generous offer," he said formally. "However, he must decline. He insists that you remain in your suite until the situation is resolved, for your own safety."

Kate had expected this answer, had known Devon would refuse to use her in this way, especially given his careful respect for her boundaries despite their captive-captor relationship. His refusal only strengthened her resolve. "Take me to him," she said, her tone allowing for no argument. "He can refuse in person."

Marcus looked as if he might object, then sighed with the weariness of someone who had served a stubborn master for too long to be surprised by similar traits in others. "Very well," he conceded. "But I must warn you, his condition has deteriorated in the past hour. He's experiencing physical agony that would kill a human, but his immortal body won't allow him the mercy. It could be dangerous for you."

Kate nodded, steeling herself for whatever awaited her. Marcus led her through corridors she had never entered before, deeper into the private wing of the house that contained Devon's personal quarters. They stopped before a heavy wooden door reinforced with what appeared to be steel bands, a door designed to keep something in rather than out.

"Last chance to reconsider," Marcus said, his hand on the door handle.

"Open it," Kate replied, her voice steadier than she felt.

Marcus unlocked the door with a key from his pocket, then stepped aside to allow Kate to enter. "I'll wait here," he said. "If you need assistance, call out immediately."

Kate nodded and stepped into Devon's private quarters. The room was dimly lit and it took a moment for Kate's eyes to adjust to the gloom. When they did, she saw a spacious chamber dominated by a large bed. Devon lay on the bed, but the composed, aristocratic man Kate knew was not there. His body wracked with violent tremors that shook the entire bed frame, his back arching as spasms coursed through him. Sweat poured from his skin, which had taken on a sickly, grayish color that made him look like a corpse. His breathing came in harsh, ragged gasps punctuated by low groans of pain that seemed torn from somewhere deep inside him.

"Devon," Kate said softly, approaching the bed.

His eyes snapped open at the sound of her voice, and Kate gasped involuntarily. The usual clear blue of his irises had been consumed by an unnatural brightness, the pupils contracted to pinpoints. These were the eyes of a predator, not the cultured man who had kissed her so gently the night before.

"Kate," he rasped, his voice rough with pain. "You shouldn't be here. Marcus shouldn't have brought you."

"I insisted," she replied, moving closer despite the warning in his altered eyes. "He said you're ill. That you need blood."

Devon turned his face away, as if ashamed to be seen in this state. "It will pass," he said. "The contamination will work its way out of my system eventually."

"But you're suffering," Kate said, sitting carefully on the edge of the bed. "And it could be hours before your usual supply arrives."

Up close, she could see the extent of his suffering; dark veins had become visible beneath his pale skin, spreading like a web of poison through his system. His hands, usually so steady and controlled, shook uncontrollably. This was a creature of immense power reduced to helpless agony, unable to die but unable to find relief.

Devon's laughed harshly, without humor. "So you've come to offer yourself as a substitute? How very sacrificial."

The bitterness in his tone caught Kate off guard. This wasn't the Devon she had come to know, the thoughtful, controlled man who appreciated art and music, and treated her with careful respect despite their unusual circumstances.

"I've come to help," she said simply.

Devon turned back to look at her, his unnatural eyes searching her face. "Why?" he demanded. "Why would you help the monster who abducted you, who keeps you prisoner? Have you finally succumbed to captivity's psychological effects, Kate?"

The accusation stung, perhaps because it echoed her own doubts, her own attempts to rationalize her growing feelings for him.

"Maybe I just don't like seeing anyone suffer when I can do something about it," she countered.

"Noble," Devon said, the word twisted with pain and skepticism. "But misguided. You don't understand what you're offering."

"Then explain it to me," Kate challenged.

Devon pushed himself up to a sitting position, the movement costing him considerable effort. "What you're proposing isn't like donating blood at a clinic, neat and clinical and detached. It's intimate, invasive. I would be taking from you directly, my mouth on your skin, my teeth breaking through. There would be pain, though I would try to minimize it. Then there are the… side effects."

"Side Effects?" Kate repeated.

"My saliva contains compounds that affect the human nervous system," Devon explained reluctantly. "They prevent pain, yes, but they also create… sensations. Pleasure, to be blunt. It ensures victims remain compliant during feeding."

The implications sent heat rushing to Kate's face. "Oh," she said inadequately.

"Yes, 'oh,'" Devon echoed, a hint of his usual dry humor surfacing despite his condition. "So you see why this is a line I've been unwilling to cross, despite… despite my feelings for you."

The admission hung in the air between them, neither acknowledging it directly but both aware of its significance.

"I still want to help," Kate said finally. "Whatever the effects, whatever it means, I'm offering freely."

Devon studied her face for a long moment, conflict evident in his expression. "Why?" he asked again, but the question was different now, less accusatory, more genuinely seeking understanding.

Kate considered her answer carefully. "Because last night at the concert, when we listened to Chopin together, when you kissed me, I felt something real. Something that has nothing to do with captivity or manipulation. And I can't reconcile that feeling with letting you suffer when I could help."

The honesty of her response seemed to affect Devon deeply. He closed his eyes briefly, as if gathering strength or resolve. The violent tremors had reduced to the occasional shiver, and his breathing had become more controlled. The conversation itself seemed to be grounding him, pulling him back from the brink of complete madness.

"If we do this," he said finally, "there are conditions. I will take only what is necessary to stabilize my condition, no more. And afterward, when I've recovered, we will discuss your future here. Including," he added, his eyes meeting hers directly, "the possibility of your departure, should that remain your wish."

Kate's breath caught. Was he offering her freedom? After all these weeks of captivity, of planning escape, was he suggesting he might simply let her go? "You would let me go?" she asked, needing to be certain she understood.

"If that is what you truly want, yes," Devon replied. "I've come to realize that keeping you here against your will negates any genuine connection between us. Whatever I feel for you—and Kate, I do feel a great deal—it means nothing if you remain my prisoner."

This changed everything. Kate had been prepared to help Devon out of compassion, out of the complicated feelings that had developed despite their circumstances. But now, with freedom potentially within reach, her motivation became more complex still. Was she helping him because she cared, or because it might ensure her release? Was she using him even as she offered to let him use her? The ethical tangle was dizzying.

"I accept your conditions," she said finally, pushing aside the moral dilemma for the moment. "What do I need to do?"

Devon's response was interrupted by another violent spasm that arched his back off the bed. His hands clawed at the sheets, and for a moment, the wild look returned to his eyes. Kate watched him struggle, fighting to regain the control he'd barely managed to grasp.

Without thinking, Kate reached out and took his hand. His fingers were ice-cold and trembling, but they immediately closed around hers with desperate strength.

"Breathe with me," she said softly, the words coming from some instinct she didn't fully understand. "Just breathe."

Devon's eyes locked onto hers, and she began to breathe slowly, deliberately. In… and out. In… and out. Gradually, impossibly, his ragged breathing began to sync with hers. The tremors in his hand lessened, though they didn't disappear entirely.

"You're my anchor," he whispered, wonder in his voice despite the pain. "In all this chaos, you're the one steady thing."

Kate squeezed his hand gently. "Then hold on to me."

They sat like that for several minutes, hands clasped, breathing together, Kate's calm presence gradually pulling Devon back from the edge of complete loss of control. She could feel the moment when the worst of the spasm passed, when his grip on her hand shifted from desperate to grateful.

"Better?" she asked quietly.

Devon nodded, his eyes clearer now, more focused. He brought their joined hands to his lips and pressed a gentle kiss to her knuckles. "Thank you."

His expression shifted, becoming more focused, more predatory, though Kate could see the tremendous effort it still cost him to maintain this control. "Come closer," he said, his voice lower but steadier now. "And choose where… where I should feed. The wrist is traditional, but the neck provides better flow."

Kate swallowed hard, the reality of what she was about to do suddenly very immediate. After a moment's hesitation, she moved closer on the bed and tilted her head slightly, exposing the side of her neck.

"Here," she said, her voice barely above a whisper.

Devon's eyes darkened at her choice, the intimacy it implied. "Are you certain?" he asked, giving her one last chance to reconsider. In answer, Kate reached out and took his hand, guiding it to her waist in a gesture of trust. "Yes," she said simply.

Devon moved with careful restraint, drawing her closer until she was seated beside him on the bed, her body turned toward his. One hand remained at her waist, the other rose to gently brush her hair away from her neck, exposing the smooth skin and the pulse that beat visibly beneath it.

"This will hurt, at first," he warned, his face now inches from her neck. "Try to relax. It will pass quickly."

Kate nodded, her eyes closing as she felt his cool breath against her skin. There was a moment of anticipation, of suspended time, and then Devon's lips pressed against her neck in what felt almost like a kiss. Her skin broke into goosebumps as a shiver ran through her. The pain when it came was sharp but brief, a quick, burning sensation as his teeth broke the skin. Kate gasped, her hand instinctively gripping his shoulder. Then, just as Devon had promised, the pain transformed into something else entirely.

Warmth spread from the point of contact, radiating through her body in waves of sensation that were not quite pleasure but adjacent to it, a languorous, floating feeling that made her limbs heavy and her thoughts hazy. She was aware of Devon's mouth against her neck, the gentle pressure as he drew her blood into himself, of his hand at her waist steadying her as she swayed slightly.

Time seemed to stretch and compress simultaneously. The experience was intimate in a way she hadn't anticipated, creating a connection that went beyond the physical act itself. She felt vulnerable yet powerful, giving life to this immortal being who held her with such careful restraint.

When Devon finally pulled away, his lips leaving her neck with what felt like reluctance, Kate found herself leaning against him, her head resting on his shoulder, her body relaxed in a way that should have alarmed her but somehow didn't.

"Kate," Devon said softly, his voice already stronger, more like himself. "Are you alright?"

She nodded against his shoulder, not yet trusting herself to speak. Devon's hand moved to stroke her hair gently, the gesture soothing and grounding as the effects of his feeding gradually receded.

"Thank you," he said, the words weighted with meaning beyond simple gratitude. "What you've given me… it's more than you know."

Kate lifted her head to look at him, noting the change in his appearance. The ashen pallor had faded, replaced by a healthier tone. His eyes, while still unnaturally bright, had lost the predatory intensity of before. "You look better," she observed, her voice slightly hoarse.

"I feel better," Devon confirmed. "The fresh blood is already purging the contamination. By tomorrow, I should be fully recovered."

Kate nodded, pleased by his improvement yet uncertain about what had just transpired between them. The intimacy of the feeding, combined with Devon's promise to discuss her potential release, had created a new complexity in their already complicated relationship.

"You should rest now," Devon said, helping her to stand. "The effects of the feeding will leave you tired, possibly lightheaded. Marcus will escort you back to your suite."

Kate wanted to protest, to stay and talk through the implications of what had just happened, but she could feel fatigue settling into her bones, a heaviness that made even standing an effort. "We'll talk tomorrow?" she asked. She needed to know that his offer of freedom hadn't been a delirious promise.

"Tomorrow," Devon agreed, his eyes holding hers with new intensity. "We have much to discuss."

Marcus appeared at the door as if summoned, his expression carefully neutral, though his eyes widened slightly at the sight of Kate's neck. Devon must have noticed, because he reached out and gently adjusted the collar of her shirt to cover the marks his feeding had left. "Take care of her, Marcus," Devon instructed, his tone making it clear that Kate's wellbeing was an absolute priority.

Kate leaned heavily on Marcus's arm for support as they left Devon's room. Her mind was all over the place, she had come to help Devon out of compassion, because of the genuine connection that had developed between them. She had not expected him to offer her freedom in return, nor had she anticipated the sensual intimacy of the feeding experience.

Now, with her escape plan with Mira still in place for Thursday and Devon's promise of potential release hanging between them, Kate faced a choice she had never expected to make: To flee or to wait, to trust or to take matters into her own hands.

As Marcus helped her into her bed, concern evident in his usually impassive features, Kate closed her eyes against the complexity of her situation. Tomorrow, she would have to decide, continue with her plan to escape with Mira, or trust Devon's offer to discuss her release. Tomorrow, she would have to confront the feelings that had developed between them, feelings that the feeding had only intensified.

Tomorrow. For now, exhaustion claimed her, pulling her into a deep sleep filled with dreams of music and art, freedom and captivity, a gentle kiss and the more primal connection of teeth against skin.

Chapter 9

Thursday morning was a perfect sunny day that seemed to mock the weight of Kate's impending decision. She had slept poorly, her dreams a kaleidoscope of conflicting images, Devon's face as he offered her freedom, the estate gates opening to release her, his lips against her neck in that moment of deep connection when she had saved his life.

She put on pants, a shirt, and running shoes that would allow for easy, flexible movement. Her neck still had faint marks where his fangs had pierced into her skin, a reminder of the intimate moment they had shared when he was most vulnerable. Yet here she was, about to betray the trust that had grown between them.

In her pocket was the promised payment. Necklaces, rings, earrings were carefully packed to prevent too much notice. Their weight represented a choice that would ultimately alter whatever fragile understanding she and Devon had reached.

At 9:10 AM, Kate positioned herself along her usual walking path, her heart hammering with anticipation and uncertainty. The white delivery van arrived on schedule, and Kate watched as the familiar routine of unloading began. Mira was there with her clipboard, efficiently directing the process while occasionally checking her watch, a new detail that suggested she was aware of the timing of their plan.

Kate approached casually, maintaining the pretense of a morning walk for any watching staff. When she reached Mira, she offered a friendly greeting that would appear normal to observers. "Good morning," she said. "Beautiful day, isn't it?"

Mira nodded, her expression carefully neutral though her eyes were alert and questioning. "Perfect weather," she agreed. "Did you bring another sketch for me to look at?"

"I did Kate replied, lowering her voice. "Would you like to take a look?" She slipped the bags of jewelry from her pockets, passing them to Mira under the pretence of showing her something in her sketchbook. Mira tucked them away smoothly into the interior pockets of her jacket, her movements practiced and inconspicuous.

"The van will be parked here for twenty minutes," Mira murmured, her eyes on her clipboard. "I'll leave the keys in the ignition and walk to the storage building to check inventory. There's a delivery uniform in the passenger seat. Change quickly and drive out normally. The gate opens automatically for the van."

Kate nodded slightly, her decision crystallizing in this moment of concrete planning. "Thank you," she whispered. "I won't forget this."

Mira's eyes met hers briefly. "Don't come back to this area," she warned. "Mr Karlov has many connections, get as far away as possible."

The warning sent a chill through Kate, reminding her exactly what Devon was, despite the gentleness he had shown her. She nodded again, then continued her walk. Kate circled the grounds, gradually working her way back toward the service entrance while appearing to simply enjoy the gardens. Her mind was plagued with second thoughts and justifications. Even though Devon had offered freedom, even with the connection that had grown between them, freedom on her own terms, taken rather than granted, called to something fundamental in her nature.

And if a small voice whispered that she was betraying a trust, breaking a connection that had become meaningful to them both, well, she silenced it firmly. Freedom was worth any price, even the loss of whatever had begun to grow between them.

When Kate saw Mira leave the van and walk toward the storage building, clipboard in hand, she knew it was time. Moving with casual purpose, she approached the service area, glancing around to ensure no staff were watching closely. The loading had been completed, the estate workers returned to their duties. The moment was perfect.

Kate slipped into the driver's seat of the van, her heart pounding so loudly she was certain it must be audible. The keys were in the ignition as promised, and a delivery uniform lay folded on the passenger seat. Working quickly, she pulled the uniform shirt over her own clothes, tucked her hair up under the cap, and adjusted it to partially obscure her face.

The engine started with a quiet rumble, and Kate took a deep breath, steeling herself for what came next. She had driven in Europe before, though not recently, and never a delivery van. But the principles were the same, and the service gate was only a short distance away.

Putting the van in gear, Kate began to drive slowly toward the exit, maintaining a casual pace that wouldn't attract attention. In her rearview mirror, she could see Mira emerging from the storage building, her expression carefully blank as she watched the van depart.

The service gate loomed ahead, its heavy metal barrier the final obstacle between captivity and freedom. Kate held her breath as she approached, half-expecting alarms to sound or security personnel to appear. But the gate began to open automatically, responding to the van's approach just as Mira had promised.

Exhilaration rushed through Kate as the van passed through the opening. She had done it, she had escaped the estate, outwitted Devon's security, reclaimed her freedom through her own actions. The narrow service road stretched before her, winding down from the estate toward the main highway. Kate accelerated slightly, eager to put distance between herself and captivity. In her mind, she was already planning her next steps: Drive to Budapest, abandon the van, sell the remaining jewelry to get cash, get to the airport and fly out of the country.

Unlike her previous attempts at visualizing escape, this time the plan was unfolding perfectly. No one had stopped her. No dark figure stood in the road ahead. She was free.

* * *

Four hours later, Kate sat in the departure lounge at Budapest Ferenc Liszt International Airport, a small carry-on bag beside her containing the few possessions she had managed to purchase after trading several pieces of jewelry from Devon's estate at a city pawnshop. She had abandoned the delivery van in a shopping center parking lot, changed out of the uniform in a public restroom, and taken a taxi to the airport.

Her remaining cash had been enough to secure a one-way ticket to London. From there, she would figure out her next steps. Contact the American embassy, explain that she had lost her passport while traveling, arrange for emergency documentation to return to New York. The details were hazy, but the immediate goal was clear: Get as far from Hungary and Devon Karlov as possible.

As her flight was called for boarding, Kate joined the queue, passport and boarding pass in hand. The document wasn't her own, it was one Mira had provided as part of their arrangement, belonging to a cousin with similar features. It wasn't ideal, but it would have to do until she could get proper identification.

The boarding process went smoothly, the harried gate agent barely glancing at her face as she scanned the boarding pass and waved Kate through. On the plane, Kate found her window seat near the middle of the economy section and settled in, allowing herself to breathe fully for what felt like the first time in hours.

She had done it. She had escaped. In less than three hours, she would be in London, beyond Devon's immediate reach. The thought brought both exhilaration and an unexpected pang of something like regret, which she quickly suppressed.

As the last passengers boarded and the cabin crew prepared for departure, Kate leaned her head against the window, watching the activity on the tarmac below. The adrenaline that had carried her through the morning was beginning to ebb, leaving her exhausted but wary, unable to fully relax until the plane was airborne.

The captain's voice came over the intercom, welcoming passengers and announcing an on-time departure. The safety demonstration began, flight attendants moving through their practiced routine as Kate half-watched, her mind already racing ahead to London, to freedom, to the life she would reclaim.

The plane had just begun to push back from the gate when Kate noticed a commotion at the front of the cabin. Two flight attendants were speaking with what appeared to be airport security personnel who had boarded the aircraft. Their conversation was too quiet to hear from her position, but the serious expressions and gesturing toward the passenger manifest sent a chill of foreboding through Kate.

It couldn't be. He couldn't have found her so quickly.

But even as she tried to reassure herself, the security officers began moving down the aisle, scanning faces, checking seat numbers. Kate sank lower in her seat, pulling a magazine from the seat pocket and opening it in front of her face in a futile attempt at concealment. The officers stopped beside her row, and Kate knew without looking up that she had been found.

"Ms Morgan?" one of them said in accented English. "Please come with us."

Kate considered her options in a flash of desperate calculation. Create a scene? Refuse to move? Claim mistaken identity? But the crowded plane offered no real escape route, and causing a disturbance would only make things worse.

"There must be some mistake," she tried.

"No mistake, Ms Morgan, please gather your belongings and come with us."

Curious murmurs drifted through the cabin, all eyes now on Kate as she rose and slowly reached for her small bag in the overhead compartment. The walk of shame down the aisle felt endless, each step taking her further from the freedom she had fought so hard for.

In the jet bridge, two more men waited, not airport security. Kate realized with sinking certainty that they must be Devon's people. They wore dark suits and earpieces, their expressions professionally blank as they flanked her, one taking her bag, the other placing a firm hand on her elbow to guide her movement.

They led her through the terminal via service corridors, avoiding the main concourse where her distress might attract attention. Kate walked in numb silence, her mind racing with scenarios of what awaited her. Would Devon's previous offer of freedom be rescinded? Outside, a black SUV with tinted windows waited at a private entrance.

"Get in," the man instructed, his tone leaving no room for argument as he opened the door. Kate slid into the leather seat as the door closed firmly behind her. The two men sat in the front, and the vehicle pulled away from the curb, merging into airport traffic.

The drive back to the estate passed in tense silence, Kate watching through the window as Budapest gave way to countryside, then to the familiar winding road that led to her gilded prison. With each mile, her anxiety grew, her mind picturing all the ways Devon might react.

When the SUV passed through the main gates of the estate, déjà vu washed over Kate. She had returned to the place she tried so hard to leave, like a character trapped in a bad dream. The vehicle stopped at the main entrance, where Marcus stood on the steps with a tense expression. "He's in his study," Marcus said as Kate got out of the car. "He's been waiting for hours."

The ominous statement did nothing to calm Kate's nerves as she was led through the familiar corridors to Devon's private study. Outside the heavy wooden door, Marcus paused. "He's very angry, Ms Morgan," he said quietly, a warning in his tone. "I would advise caution in how you respond."

With that, he knocked once and opened the door. He stepped aside to let Kate in before closing it behind her. Devon stood by the window, turned away from the door. The moonlight created a shadow on him. His posture was rigid, and his hands were tightly held behind him. Tension was clear in every line of his body. He didn't turn when Kate came in and didn't acknowledge her presence during the long, painful moments in the silent room. When he finally spoke, his voice was low and controlled, with an undercurrent of fury that made Kate's blood run cold.

"You made it quite far," he said, still facing the window. "Budapest. The airport. A flight to London. Impressive."

Kate remained silent, unsure if a response was expected or would only provoke his anger further.

"Do you have any idea," Devon continued, turning slowly to face her, "what resources I had to expend to find you so quickly? What favors I had to call in? The attention I had to draw to myself?"

His eyes were cold, his expression harder than Kate had ever seen it. This was not the cultured, controlled man she had come to know, nor the vulnerable being who had fed from her during his illness. This was something older, darker, the predator beneath the civilized veneer.

"I'm sorry," Kate said, the words inadequate but all she could offer.

"Sorry?" Devon repeated, a harsh laugh escaping him. "Sorry for what, exactly? For attempting to escape? For betraying my trust? Or merely for getting caught?"

He moved toward her with unnatural speed, suddenly standing right in front of her. She had to tilt her head back to maintain eye contact. "I offered you freedom," he said, each word clear and sharp. "A clean break. I offered you the choice to leave or stay. And you chose deception and theft instead."

"I needed to leave on my terms, not yours," Kate replied, finding her voice despite her fear. "I couldn't be sure your offer was genuine."

"So you've said before," Devon countered. "And yet, here we are, you, having fled at the first opportunity; me, having expended considerable resources to retrieve you."

He turned away abruptly, moving to his desk where a glass of what appeared to be whiskey sat untouched. He lifted it, then set it down again without drinking. "Mira will have to be dealt with, of course, her betrayal is perhaps more significant than yours, given her family's long association with mine."

Kate's heart stuttered at the implication. "Dealt with? What does that mean?"

Devon's smile was cold. "What do you think it means, Kate? She helped your escape, took payment to betray me. There are consequences for such actions in my world."

"No," Kate said, stepping forward without thinking. "Please, don't hurt her. She was just doing what I asked, what I paid her to do. If anyone should be punished, it's me."

Devon studied her, something calculating in his gaze. "You would take her punishment? Interesting. What exactly are you offering, Kate?"

The question hung in the air between them, loaded with implication. Kate swallowed hard, gathering her courage.

"Whatever punishment you planned for her," she said. "Give it to me instead. She was just trying to help someone she thought was being held against their will."

"And you were being held against your will," Devon pointed out. "Despite my offer of freedom, the connection that had grown between us, you still saw yourself as my prisoner."

Kate couldn't deny it, not entirely. "I saw myself as someone who needed to reclaim agency," she corrected. "To leave on my terms, not yours."

Devon was silent for a long moment, considering her words. Then he moved back to the window, his back to her once more. "Go to your room, Kate," he said finally, his voice weary rather than angry now. "We'll discuss this further tomorrow."

The dismissal was unexpected after the intensity of his initial fury. Kate hesitated, uncertain if she had truly deflected his anger from Mira or simply postponed the issue. "Mira?" she pressed. "You won't punish her?"

Devon sighed, a sound that seemed to carry the weight of centuries. "Your concern for her is noted. Go to your room, Kate. Now."

Something in his tone suggested she not push any further argument. Kate turned and left the study, relief mingling with apprehension as she made her way to her suite. Had she succeeded in protecting Mira? Had Devon's anger burned itself out, or was he merely regrouping before delivering consequences?

In her rooms, everything was exactly as she had left it that morning, a lifetime ago, it seemed. Kate moved through the familiar space in a daze, the events of the day catching up with her in a wave of exhaustion. She had been so close to freedom, had tasted it briefly before being dragged back to captivity.

And yet, a small voice whispered, was it truly captivity when Devon had offered her freedom? When he had been prepared to let her go with his blessing and support? Her escape attempt suddenly seemed foolish rather than brave.

Kate showered and changed into nightclothes, moving through the familiar routine while her mind processed. No one came to bring her dinner and she didn't dare leave her suite to seek food, uncertain of her status in the household after the day's events.

Eventually Kate fell into a restless sleep, her dreams filled with airports and roads that led in circles, always returning to the estate, to Devon.

***

She woke with a start to find Marcus standing beside her bed, his expression grim in the dim light of early dawn. "Get up," he said without preamble. "Mr Karlov requires your presence."

Kate blinked, disoriented by the abrupt awakening and the unusual hour. "What time is it?"

"Nearly sunrise," Marcus replied. "There isn't much time. Come now, as you are."

The urgency in his tone propelled Kate from bed, quickly pulling on a robe over her nightgown. Marcus didn't wait for her to find slippers or fix her hair, already moving toward the door with an expectation that she would follow.

They moved through the quiet house, the early morning light just beginning to filter through windows as they descended to the lower levels, then through corridors Kate had never seen before. The path was taking them deeper into the private wing that contained Devon's quarters, she realized with growing unease.

"Where are we going?" she asked, her voice echoing slightly in the empty hallway.

Marcus didn't answer, continuing his brisk pace until they reached the heavy door to Devon's personal quarters. He unlocked it with a key from his pocket, gesturing for Kate to enter ahead of him. The outer chamber was dimly lit, but Kate could see Devon standing by the concealed door that led to his sleeping chamber, a circular room with a recessed bed and the stone slab that sealed it during daylight hours. His expression was unreadable as he watched her approach.

"What's happening?" Kate asked, looking between Devon and Marcus with apprehension.

"Your punishment," Devon said simply. "For your escape attempt and the trouble it caused."

Kate's heart raced as understanding dawned. "The sleeping chamber, you're going to lock me in there?"

"With me," Devon clarified. "Dawn approaches, and I must retire to my sanctuary. You will join me."

The implication sent a wave of panic through Kate. "For how long?"

"Until sunset," Devon replied. "And every day hereafter, until I decide the lesson has been learned."

Kate took an instinctive step backward, only to find Marcus blocking her retreat. "You can't be serious," she said, her voice rising. "Locked in that tomb for an entire day? I'll suffocate!"

"The chamber has ventilation," Devon said calmly. "You will be uncomfortable, perhaps frightened, but not in physical danger."

"Please," Kate said, desperation creeping into her tone. "Any other punishment. Not that."

Devon's expression softened slightly, a flicker of regret crossing his features before the mask of determination returned. "You offered to take Mira's punishment. This is it. The alternative is her dismissal from the estate and the withdrawal of my protection from her family, protection they have relied upon for generations."

The choice was clear, though it felt like no choice at all. Kate looked toward the sleeping chamber door, then back at Devon, seeing the resolve in his stance. "Fine," she said finally, her voice small but steady. "I'll do it."

Devon nodded once, then turned towards the bed chamber. "After you," Devon said, gesturing for Kate to enter.

With heavy steps, Kate moved past him into the chamber, its cool air raising goosebumps on her skin. The recessed bed looked even more like a tomb in the dim light, the burgundy sheets a stark contrast to the stone surroundings. Devon followed her in, closing the door behind them with a finality that made Kate's breath catch. They were alone now, sealed in this ancient space designed to protect a vampire during his most vulnerable hours.

"The slab will descend soon," Devon said, moving to the edge of the recessed area. "An automatic timer triggered by the approaching dawn. I suggest you make yourself as comfortable as possible."

Kate remained standing, arms wrapped around herself as she watched Devon remove his shoes and outer clothing, leaving him in a t-shirt and boxers. The domesticity of the action felt surreal in the moment. "Please," she tried one more time, her voice breaking. "Don't do this. Let me out."

Devon paused, looking at her with a mix of determination and regret. "You chose this, Kate. When you tried to escape despite my offer of freedom, when you got Mira involved in your plans, when you volunteered to take her punishment, you chose this path."

A mechanical sound above caught Kate's attention. She looked up at the ceiling where the massive stone slab had started to descend slowly. Panic surged through her. Claustrophobia she hadn't realized she had rose up like a wave. "No!" she shouted, rushing to the door and pulling desperately at the handle. "Let me out! Please!"

Devon made no move to stop her, watching with ancient eyes as she rattled the door that would not open, as she searched frantically for some override to the descending slab. "Marcus!" she shouted, pounding on the door. "Help me! Don't let him do this!"

But there was no response from beyond the sealed door, no rescue coming as the stone slab continued its inexorable descent. Kate turned back to Devon, tears streaming down her face now.

"Please," she begged. "I'm sorry. I'm so sorry. Don't lock me in here."

Devon's expression softened slightly at her distress. "It's too late to stop the mechanism," he said. "And even if it weren't, this is necessary, Kate. You need to understand that actions have consequences. Trust, once broken, is difficult to repair."

The slab was halfway down now, the space in the chamber growing more confined with each passing second. Kate felt her breathing accelerate, panic making her light-headed as the walls seemed to close in around her.

"I can't," she gasped, sliding down against the door to sit on the floor, knees pulled up to her chest. "I can't do this."

Devon moved toward her then, crouching to meet her at eye level. "You can," he said, his voice gentler now. "And you will. I'll be right here with you."

"How is that supposed to help?" Kate demanded, anger flaring through her fear. "You'll be unconscious while I'm trapped in this tomb!"

"Not immediately," Devon corrected. "The lethargy takes time to set in. I'll be with you until then."

The slab continued its descent, now just feet above their heads. Kate's panic reached a crescendo, her breathing coming in short, sharp gasps as the reality of her situation became inescapable.

"Come," Devon said, extending his hand to her. "The bed is more comfortable than the floor."

Kate ignored his offered hand, remaining huddled against the door as the slab lowered further, forcing Devon to duck his head as he moved to the recessed bed. He settled onto it, watching her with a mixture of determination and concern.

"This isn't how I imagined you coming to my bed," he said quietly. "Is this what you think I wanted, Kate? To force you into my sleeping chamber, to see you terrified and weeping?"

The question penetrated Kate's panic, drawing her attention to the genuine regret in Devon's expression. "Then why?" she managed between gasping breaths. "Why do this?"

"Because you need to understand what trust means to someone like me," Devon replied. "Because you need to experience the vulnerability I face every day when I place my life in the hands of others during my dormancy."

The slab was now just inches above Kate's head, the confined space making her panic spike again. With a final sob, she scrambled away from the door and into the recessed area, as far from Devon as the limited space would allow. The stone slab completed its descent with a final, heavy sound, sealing them in complete darkness for a moment before dim lighting activated around the perimeter of the recessed area. The space was now entirely enclosed, a vault designed to protect its occupant from deadly sunlight.

Kate curled into herself at the edge of the bed, as far from Devon as possible, her body shaking with silent sobs. The reality of being sealed in this underground chamber for an entire day was overwhelming, her claustrophobia a living thing clawing at her chest.

"Breathe, Kate," Devon's voice came through the dimness. "Slow, deep breaths. The air is circulating. You're safe."

"Safe?" Kate repeated, a hysterical edge to her laughter. "Locked in an underground tomb with a vampire? How is that safe?"

"I would never harm you," Devon said, his voice steady and certain. "Despite everything, despite your escape attempt and broken trust, I care for you too much to ever cause you deliberate harm."

The sincerity in his voice penetrated Kate's panic slightly, allowing her to draw a deeper breath. She focused on the dim lights, on the sound of air moving through hidden vents, on anything but the stone slab sealing them in. "How long?" she asked, her voice small in the enclosed space.

"Until sunset," Devon replied. "Approximately twelve hours."

The prospect of twelve hours in this confined space sent another wave of anxiety through Kate, but she forced herself to breathe through it. Panic would only make the time pass more slowly, would only make the experience more unbearable.

"Try to sleep," Devon suggested. "The time will pass more quickly."

"Sleep?" Kate repeated incredulously. "How am I supposed to sleep in this… this coffin?"

Devon sighed, the sound weary in the dim light. "It's not a coffin, Kate. It's a sanctuary. A place of safety and rest."

"For you, maybe," Kate muttered, still huddled at the edge of the bed.

Silence fell between them, broken only by Kate's gradually steadying breathing and the faint sound of the ventilation system. After what might have been minutes or hours, Devon spoke again, his voice softer now.

"I am beginning to feel the lethargy," he said. "Dawn has fully arrived above."

Kate glanced at him, noting the heaviness in his limbs, the slight slurring of his words. The fearsome vampire was becoming vulnerable before her eyes, the daylight working its ancient magic even through layers of stone and earth.

"What happens now?" she asked, curiosity momentarily overriding fear.

"I will fall into dormancy soon," Devon replied, his words coming more slowly. "A state like deep sleep. I will be aware of nothing until sunset."

"And I'll be alone," Kate said, a tremor returning to her voice.

Devon's eyes, heavy-lidded now with approaching dormancy, held hers across the dim space.

"I'm sorry for that," he said, genuine regret in his tone. "But perhaps... perhaps it will help you understand... what trust means to me."

His words were becoming more disjointed, his body relaxing into the stillness of vampire dormancy. Kate watched as Devon's eyes finally closed, his breathing slowing to a standstill. She was now alone in the sealed chamber with her dormant captor next to her.

Kate drew her knees to her chest and tried to focus on her breathing. The idea of enduring hours in this underground prison was maddening.

Once the panic subsided into anxiety, Kate reflected on the events that had led her here. Her escape attempt, Devon's fury, her offer to take Mira's punishment. Had she made the right choice? Was protecting a virtual stranger worth this torment? Beside her, Devon lay in perfect stillness, vulnerable in his dormancy despite being her jailer. The contradiction was striking, this powerful being, rendered helpless by sunlight, trusting her not to harm him during his unholy sleep.

Trust. The word echoed in Kate's mind as the hours dragged on. Devon had trusted her with his life during his illness when she fed him. He had relied on her to consider his offer of freedom honestly. Now, even as he punished her for breaking that trust, he was showing the deepest trust by lying still beside her.

Kate caught the irony as she finally lay down on the bed, exhaustion overtaking her fear as time went by. As she drifted into an uneasy sleep, her last thought was that maybe this punishment held more significance than she had first realized. It was a lesson in vulnerability and trust that went deeper than mere punishment.

When she woke, it was to the sound of the stone slab beginning to rise. Devon stirred beside her as sunset neared. The day had gone by, the lesson had been learned, and Kate found herself looking at her captor with a new understanding of the complex dynamics that connected them.

Chapter 10

T he ritual quickly became routine. Each day, once evening arrived, the stone slab would rise from the tomb, allowing Kate to leave her underground prison. Devon would wake from his dormancy moments later, his eyes finding hers across the dim space as awareness returned to him.

Those first few days, Kate would run from the chamber the instant the slab lifted enough for her to slip beneath it, desperate for fresh air and open space after hours of confinement. She would spend her evenings and nights as far from Devon as possible, taking meals in her room, painting furiously in her studio, or walking the gardens under the stars, anything to avoid interaction with her captor.

But as dawn approached, Marcus would inevitably appear to escort her back to the sleeping chamber, where Devon waited with solemn eyes and few words. Each morning, Kate would position herself at the very edge of the recessed bed, maintaining maximum distance from Devon as the stone slab descended to seal them in for another day.

The hours of confinement were torture at first. Kate would curl into herself, back turned to Devon's dormant form, alternating between fitful sleep and anxious wakefulness. By the third day, exhaustion won the battle as Kate's body began to surrender to inevitable sleep. She slept longer in the chamber, her body slowly adapting to the rhythm of the ritual.

It was on the fourth day that the first significant shift occurred. Kate woke from a surprisingly deep sleep to find herself no longer at the edge of the bed but closer to its center, closer to Devon. Her body had betrayed her in sleep; it sought comfort rather than distance. She jerked away immediately, heart racing as she checked to make sure Devon remained dormant. His perfect stillness reassured her, but the incident left her shaken. Was her subconscious already adapting to this punishment, already seeking to be close to the very being who had imprisoned her?

That evening, when the slab rose and Devon awakened, Kate didn't flee immediately. Instead, she remained seated on the edge of the bed, watching as awareness returned to his features. "Why are you doing this?" she asked, the question that had been building for days finally finding voice. "What do you hope to accomplish by locking me in here with you?"

Devon sat up slowly, his movements still languid from the transition out of dormancy. "What do you think I'm trying to accomplish, Kate?"

"Punishment," she replied immediately. "Control. Reminding me that I'm your prisoner no matter what freedoms you pretend to offer."

Devon shook his head slightly, disappointment evident in his expression. "If that were my goal, there are far more effective methods available to me."

"Then what?" Kate pressed. "Why this specific punishment?"

Devon was silent for a moment, studying her with those ancient eyes that had seen centuries pass. "Trust," he said finally. "Understanding. Perspective."

"Explain," Kate demanded, unwilling to accept such vague answers after days of confinement.

"Each day, I place my life in your hands," Devon said simply. "During my dormancy, I am completely vulnerable. You could harm me, even destroy me, and I would be powerless to stop you."

The thought had occurred to Kate, of course. In those long hours of confinement, she had contemplated the strange power dynamic, how her captor became utterly defenseless for hours each day, trusting her not to take advantage of that vulnerability.

"So this is… what? A trust exercise?" she asked incredulously.

"In part," Devon acknowledged. "But it's also about perspective. You feel trapped, confined, your freedom restricted. Now you begin to understand what existence is like for me, bound by the rhythm of sun and moon, forced to retreat to underground chambers, living in the shadows while the world moves in the light."

The comparison hadn't occurred to Kate before, and it struck her with unexpected force. Devon's immortality came with its own form of captivity. A prison of sunlight and secrecy that had confined him for centuries.

"How long will this continue?" she asked, her voice softer now.

"Until I believe you understand what trust means between us," Devon replied. "Until I believe you won't attempt escape again."

"And if I promise that now?" Kate tried.

Devon's smile was sad but knowing. "Words are easy, Kate. Understanding is harder. It takes time." With that, he rose and left the chamber, leaving Kate to think about his words and the days of confinement still ahead.

A week passed, then another. The daily ritual continued, confinement during daylight hours, freedom in the evenings and nights. Kate kept her distance from Devon during her waking hours, but something was shifting within her, a gradual change she couldn't entirely acknowledge even to herself.

In the chamber, she no longer huddled at the extreme edge of the bed. The space was limited, and maintaining such an uncomfortable position had proven unsustainable. She still kept distance between them, but it was a reasonable gap now rather than a desperate attempt to be as far away as possible.

More troubling was her growing awareness of Devon's presence beside her. In the early days, she had tried to ignore him completely and pretend she was alone in the chamber. Now she found herself watching him as he fell into dormancy, fascinated by the transition. She would study his features in the dim light, the strong line of his jaw, the dark sweep of his lashes against his cheek, the slight furrow between his brows that persisted even in dormancy.

These observations disturbed her, evidence of an interest she tried to deny. She told herself it was simply the result of proximity and boredom, there was little else to look at in the tight space, after all. But the justification rang hollow even to her own ears.

The most significant shift came on the fifteenth day of her punishment. Kate had been sleeping poorly the night before, troubled by dreams she couldn't quite remember upon waking. When Marcus came to escort her to the chamber at dawn, she was already exhausted, her defenses lowered by fatigue.

In the chamber, Devon noticed her state immediately. "You're tired," he observed as the slab began its descent.

"Bad dreams," Kate replied curtly, taking her usual position on the bed. Devon nodded, settling into his own space without further comment.

As the slab completed its descent and the dim emergency lighting activated, Kate felt the familiar wave of claustrophobia wash over her, though weaker now than in those first terrible days.

"Try to rest," Devon said, his voice already slowing as dormancy approached. "The day will pass more quickly if you sleep."

Kate didn't respond, curling onto her side with her back to him as was her habit. But sleep proved elusive despite her exhaustion, her mind racing with fragmented thoughts and lingering unease from her d Reams Hours passed in restless half-sleep. A particularly vivid flash of her nightmare returned, something about being lost and running down endless corridors that led nowhere. Kate gasped and sat up abruptly in the dimly lit chamber. She turned to Devon, seeking reassurance from another presence, even a dormant one. His stillness was somehow comforting, serving as a constant in the disorienting space.

Kate found herself moving closer, drawn by an impulse she didn't fully understand, and settled beside him. The proximity should have disturbed her, should have triggered alarm bells. Instead, it brought a strange sense of calm, slowing her racing heart and steadying her breathing. "This doesn't mean anything," she whispered to his unhearing form. "It's just... easier this way."

Even as she spoke the words, Kate knew they weren't entirely true. Something was changing within her, had been changing gradually since that first night in the chamber. The daily ritual of confinement, of witnessing Devon's vulnerability and sharing this most intimate of spaces, was affecting her in ways she hadn't anticipated and couldn't entirely control.

She fell asleep beside him, closer than she had ever voluntarily been during their daylight confinement. When she woke hours later, she found herself curled against his side with her head resting on his shoulder and an arm draped across his chest in a position of intimate trust that would have been unthinkable just days before.

Kate moved away immediately, heart pounding with confusion and something like shame. What was happening to her? How could she seek comfort from the very person who had imprisoned her, who forced her into this underground chamber day after day?

The rational part of her mind supplied the answer readily enough: Stockholm Syndrome, trauma bonding, the psychological adaptation of captives to their captors. She had heard about such phenomena and understood the mechanisms behind them. But understanding didn't make the experience any less real or confusing.

The third week of Kate's punishment brought a development she could no longer deny. The daily ritual continued, confinement during daylight, freedom in the evenings, but the nature of that confinement had fundamentally changed. Kate no longer huddled at the edge of the bed, no longer turned her back on Devon's dormant form. Instead, she had begun to settle naturally beside him as the slab descended each morning, sometimes reading from books she brought into the chamber, sometimes sketching in a small notebook, often simply resting in a companionable silence.

Kate had stopped fighting the unconscious movement that drew her to Devon's side, that sought the comfort of contact during her vulnerable hours of rest. She would wake to find herself curled against him, her head on his shoulder or chest, her arm draped across his body in a position of intimate trust that no longer shocked her.

Now, she simply accepted it, carefully extracting herself before sunset without the panic or shame that had marked her earlier responses. It was easier not to examine these changes too closely, to justify them with the practical realities of confined space and the body's natural seeking of comfort during sleep.

But on the twenty-first day of her punishment, the pretense became impossible to maintain. Kate woke from a particularly deep sleep to find herself not just beside Devon but practically entwined with him, her head on his chest, her leg thrown over his, her arm wrapped around his torso as if to keep him close. The position was unmistakably intimate, but what shocked her more was her response to it. It felt right, like it was exactly where her body belonged. For long moments, Kate remained perfectly still, absorbing the sensation of being so close to Devon, of the strange peace it brought despite everything that had happened between them.

"This is insanity," she whispered to herself as she carefully unwrapped her limbs from Devon. "Textbook Stockholm Syndrome."

But even as she said the words, she knew deep down that what she felt had been developing for some time now. It was rooted in their shared appreciation of the arts, in the vulnerability they had both displayed, in the complex connection that had formed despite the circumstances of their meeting.

That evening, when the slab rose and Devon awakened, Kate didn't immediately move away as had become her habit. Instead, she remained beside him, watching as awareness returned to his features, as his eyes found hers in the dim light.

"Kate?" he questioned, surprise evident in his tone at her continued proximity.

"We need to talk," she said simply.

Devon sat up slowly, maintaining the careful distance he had established since her punishment began. "About what?"

"About this," Kate gestured to the chamber around them, to the bed they shared during daylight hours. "About what's happening to me. To us."

Devon's expression remained carefully neutral, though something flickered in his eyes at her words. "What do you think is happening, Kate?"

"I think I have feelings for you," she said directly, the confession terrifying, yet liberating. "That it might be Stockholm Syndrome, but I also think…" she hesitated, then continued with determined honesty, "I also think it might be real. That it might have started before all this, during those evenings of art and music, during the feeding when you were ill."

Devon was silent for a long moment, his ancient eyes studying her face with an intensity that might once have made her uncomfortable but now felt familiar, almost welcome. "The distinction matters to you," he observed finally. "Whether your feelings are a response to captivity or something more genuine."

"Of course it matters," Kate replied, a hint of frustration in her tone. "One is a psychological survival mechanism, a false emotion created by trauma. The other is..." she trailed off, uncertain how to complete the thought.

"Real?" Devon supplied. "Authentic? Valid?"

"Yes," Kate exhaled. "Exactly."

Devon shifted slightly, turning to face her more directly. "And if I told you that the distinction is less clear than you might think? That emotions born of difficult circumstances are not necessarily less authentic than those developed in ideal conditions?"

The suggestion challenged Kate's neat categorization, her attempt to separate "real" feelings from those induced by her captivity. "What are you saying?"

"I'm saying that human emotions are complex, Kate," Devon replied. "That they rarely fit into the tidy boxes psychology textbooks might suggest. That feelings developed during captivity might be influenced by circumstance, but not necessarily invalidated by it."

Kate considered his words, finding in them both comfort and new confusion. "So you think what I'm feeling could be real, even if it started because of... all this?" She gestured again to their surroundings.

"I think," Devon said carefully, "that what matters most is not how feelings begin but what we choose to do with them once we recognize them."

The statement was loaded with implication and possibility. Kate found herself studying Devon's face, seeing in it not just the captor who had abducted her and punished her escape attempt, but also the man who had shared art and music with her, who had offered her freedom before she fled, who had placed himself in a position of vulnerability beside her day after day.

"What would you choose to do?" she asked finally, the question both specific and expansive.

Devon's expression softened, something like hope flickering in his eyes. "If you're asking whether I have feelings for you, Kate, the answer is yes. Feelings that have grown despite my better judgment, despite knowing the problematic nature of our beginning. And if you're asking what I would choose to do about those feelings," he continued, "I would choose to acknowledge them honestly while recognizing that any relationship between us would be fundamentally complicated by how we began, by abduction and captivity, by the inherent power imbalance between us."

His honesty surprised Kate, challenging her half-formed fantasies of simple resolution. "So where does that leave us?" she asked.

"At a crossroads," Devon replied. "One where we must decide whether or not to explore what exists between us despite its problematic origins"

Kate hadn't expected such a clear assessment of their situation. "Which would you choose?" she pressed, needing to understand his position before revealing more of her own thoughts.

Devon remained silent for a long time, choosing his words carefully. "I would choose to explore what exists between us, but only under certain conditions."

"What conditions?" Kate asked, both wary and curious.

"That your punishment ends immediately," Devon said, his tone firm. "That you are free to come and go from the estate as you wish, with no restrictions or surveillance. That you have the financial means to establish independence should you choose it. In short, that the power imbalance between us is minimized as much as possible."

The offer was unexpected, a complete reversal of the punishment that had defined their relationship for weeks. "You would end all this?" Kate gestured to the chamber. "Just like that?"

"Yes," Devon confirmed. "Because any genuine relationship must be founded on choice, not coercion."

The echo of his earlier offer of freedom, the one Kate had rejected in favor of her ill-fated escape attempt, wasn't lost on her. But this time, the context was different.

"And if I chose to leave?" she asked, testing the boundaries of his offer. "If

I took that freedom and never returned?"

Pain flickered across Devon's features, but he didn't hesitate. "Then that would be your choice to make," he said simply. "And I would respect it, as I promised before."

The sincerity in his voice was unmistakable, and Kate found herself believing him despite everything that had happened between them. This was not the manipulative offer of a captor seeking to keep control, but the genuine proposal of someone who had come to care for her and recognize the fundamental problems in their beginning.

"I need time," Kate said finally. "To think about all this, to sort through what I'm feeling and what it means."

Devon nodded, accepting her response without pressure. "Of course," he said. "Take whatever time you need. But know that regardless of what you decide about us, your punishment ends tonight. You will not return to this chamber unless it is by your own choice."

The declaration brought unexpected tears to Kate's eyes, tears of relief, of confusion, of the complex emotions that had been building within her over the past few weeks. Devon reached out hesitantly, his hand hovering near hers in a gesture that asked permission rather than assuming it.

Kate looked at his outstretched hand, at the being who had been her captor and might yet become something else entirely. After a moment's hesitation, she placed her hand in his. It was a small gesture of trust, acknowledging the connection that had formed between them against all odds.

"Thank you," she said simply, the words encompassing both his offer of freedom and his honesty about the feelings that had developed between them.

Devon's fingers gently linked with hers, sending a current of warmth through Kate's body. "Whatever you decide, Kate," he whispered softly, "I want you to know that these weeks with you have changed me. You've reminded me what it means to connect and feel, to see the world through new eyes."

The declaration touched Kate. For the first time since her abduction, she felt like she finally had genuine freedom of choice. When they left the chamber together that evening, Kate felt both the weight of the decision before her and a strange lightness. Whatever came next, she would face it not as a prisoner, but as a woman making her own choices, for better or worse.

Chapter 11

The first pale light of dawn was creeping across the estate grounds when Kate made her decision. She had spent three sleepless nights wrestling with her feelings, pacing her suite, staring out at the gardens, trying to reconcile her heart with her mind. But as the sun began to rise on the fourth day, clarity struck her like lightning.

She didn't hesitate. Didn't second-guess herself. Didn't even bother to change from the silk nightgown she'd been wearing as she paced. Kate strode through the corridors with purpose, her bare feet silent on the marble floors, her heart hammering with the weight of what she was about to do.

The door to Devon's chamber swung open silently, and Kate stepped inside without pause, letting it seal behind her with its familiar soft click. Devon was in the center of the circular chamber, caught in the vulnerable moment of preparing for dormancy. His shirt lay discarded on a chair, revealing the marble perfection of his torso, and he was in the process of removing his belt when he sensed her presence. He turned, shock replacing the drowsy lethargy that had been settling over his features.

"Kate?" His voice was rough with approaching dormancy, confusion evident in his ancient eyes. "What are you—"

"I've decided," she said simply, cutting him off as she moved deeper into the chamber. The stone slab above was already beginning its slow descent, responding to the rising sun. "I want to stay," she said simply. "To explore what exists between us, despite how we began."

The tension in Devon's posture eased slightly, though his expression remained guarded. "You're certain?" he asked. "This isn't a choice to be made lightly, Kate. Our complicated beginning won't simply disappear because we want it to."

"I know," Kate acknowledged. "I've thought about little else these past days. About whether what I feel is real or merely a psychological response to captivity."

"And your conclusion?" Devon asked, his voice carefully controlled.

"That I can't know with absolute certainty," Kate admitted. "But what I feel, the connection between us, feels too significant to dismiss."

Devon's expression cycled through a dozen emotions, disbelief, hope, desire, and something deeper that she couldn't quite put her finger on. "The sun is rising," he said weakly, as if that could somehow change what she had just declared. "I need to enter dormancy."

"I know," Kate replied, reaching him now, close enough to feel the cool emanation of his skin. "That's why I'm here. I want to be with you when you sleep. I want to be here when you wake."

Devon's eyes widened with genuine surprise "After everything that happened there?"

"Because of everything that happened there," Kate corrected. "It's where I first began to understand you, where I first acknowledged what was developing between us, despite all rational objections."

The stone slab continued its descent, the chamber growing dimmer as the sun climbed higher outside. Devon's movements were becoming heavier, the ancient rhythm of his existence asserting itself despite the extraordinary circumstances.

"Come," Kate said, taking his hand and leading him toward the recessed bed. "Let's not waste what time we have."

They stepped down into the sleeping area together, Kate could see the lethargy beginning to claim him, the way his eyelids grew heavy and the slight slurring of his words.

They settled on the bed facing each other, the space between them charged with possibility. Kate's hand reached out to trace the strong line of Devon's jaw, marveling at the way he leaned into her touch like a man starved for affection.

"Tell me something," she said softly as the chamber grew darker around them. "Something you've never told anyone else."

When he finally spoke, his voice was barely above a whisper. "I had two little sisters," he murmured, his voice growing thick with more than just approaching dormancy. "When I was human. They were…they were everything to me after our parents died. I was supposed to protect them."

Kate's breath caught at the pain in his voice. "What happened to them?"

Devon's eyes drifted closed, but she could see the tension in his jaw, the way his hands clenched slightly. "Elisabeta kept me for decades. When I finally escaped, when I finally made it back…" His voice broke slightly. "They had grown old. Lived their entire lives. Died. While I remained frozen in time, they lived and died without me."

Kate felt tears prick her eyes at the raw anguish in this confession. Her fingers threaded through his dark hair, offering what comfort she could. "I'm so sorry."

"It's the story of my kind," he said quietly, "The people I care about grow old and die. Again and again." His eyes remained closed, but there was a weary acceptance in his tone that spoke of losses too numerous to count.

Kate remained silent for some time before lifting his hand to press a gentle kiss to his knuckles. "Thank you for sharing this with me," she whispered.

Devon's lips curved in the faintest of smiles at her tenderness, his breathing already growing deeper as the lethargy claimed him. The slab sealed above them with a soft thud, plunging the chamber into the profound darkness that Devon needed for his rest. But Kate wasn't afraid. She settled to him, her body curving naturally against his as his breathing deepened into the stillness of vampiric dormancy.

"Sleep," she whispered as he succumbed to the lethargy. "I'll be here when you wake."

* * *

Devon returned to consciousness gradually as the sun set. The slab above had already begun to rise, triggered by the evening light filtering into the chamber. But something was different this time, there was a warmth against his side, a weight across his chest, a scent of lavender and paint that had become uniquely Kate in his mind.

He opened his eyes to find her still asleep beside him, her body entwined with his in unconscious intimacy, her head resting on his chest, her arm draped across his torso, her leg thrown over his in a position of complete trust. Her features were relaxed in sleep, free of the wariness that had defined her for so long.

Devon didn't move a muscle for fear he might disturb her rest. Instead, he savored the moment of unguarded closeness. This was not the proximity born of punishment, but the natural seeking of comfort and connection.

As if sensing his awakening, Kate stirred, her eyes fluttering open to meet his. For a moment, confusion clouded her features, disorientated from waking in an unexpected position. Then memory returned, and with it, awareness of their entwined bodies.

In the past, such awareness had sent Kate scrambling away, embarrassed and conflicted by her unconscious seeking of comfort from her captor. This time, she remained where she was, her eyes holding Devon's in the dim light, acknowledging the intimacy of their position without shame or retreat.

A question formed in Devon's eyes, unspoken but clear in the slight tilt of his head, the careful stillness of his body. The seconds felt like eternity before Kate answered with the smallest of nods, a permission granted without words, but unmistakable in its clarity.

Devon's hand rose slowly, giving her the chance to back away. When she remained still, watching him with trust and anticipation, his fingers brushed her cheek gently. Kate's eyes closed briefly at the contact, a small sigh escaping her lips. When she looked at him again, something had shifted in her expression, a decision made, a boundary crossed in clear-eyed choice.

She raised her own hand to mirror his, fingers tracing the line of his jaw with timid exploration. Devon remained still beneath her touch, allowing her to set the pace of this new intimacy and establish the boundaries of what would happen between them. Their gazes held, a silent communication passing between them that needed no words to understand its meaning.

In Devon's eyes, a question; in Kate's, an answer. In both, a recognition of the extraordinary journey that had brought them to this moment, from abduction to captivity to punishment to chosen intimacy.

Kate shifted slightly, bringing her face closer to his, her intention clear in the parting of her lips, the question in her eyes and they darted from his to his lips. Devon remained still, allowing her to close the final distance between them, to make the choice that would transform their relationship yet again.

When their lips met, it was not the hesitant kiss outside her door after the concert. It wasn't a captor desperately claiming his captive. It was a curious, sensual exploration. His arm tightened around her waist to draw her closer without presumption. The kiss deepened gradually and Kate's body shifted against Devon's in an unconscious movement that expressed desire. Devon tentatively sucked on Kate's lower lip, savoring its fullness. His tongue massaged hers, and she returned in kind.

He responded to her cues with patience acquired over centuries, allowing the moment to unfold at its natural pace rather than rush toward conclusion. His hand traced the curve of her spine through the fabric of her clothing, a touch that offered pleasure without demand.

When they separated, it was only to look into each other's eyes, to confirm the mutual desire and consent that guided their interaction. Kate's expression held wonder and certainty in equal measure, the wonder of discovering connection where she had least expected it, the certainty that this was her choice, freely made despite the complicated path that had led them here.

Devon's eyes asked another question as his hand paused at the hem of her shirt. Kate nodded and raised her arms so he could carefully remove it. More clothing joined the shirt as they silently shed them, slowly revealing more skin. The chamber's light cast shadows across their bodies, highlighting the tension that thrummed between them. Kate's breath hitched as Devon's eyes, dark with desire, drank in her form, her curves, with hunger.

He moved above her, his weight supported by his forearms, never taking his eyes off her. Unspoken need and the quickening of their breaths filled the space. He lowered himself slowly until his body was pressed against hers, and Kate moaned, a low, desperate sound, her body arching into his, seeking the ultimate connection. Devon closed his eyes, overwhelmed not only by his own sensations but by the precious gift of Kate's pleasure, a sound so different from the cries of fear and anger that had haunted him since her arrival

His lips found hers again, a kiss that was no longer gentle exploration but desperate, a devouring hunger that consumed them both. Her mouth opened beneath his, inviting him deeper, her tongue meeting his in a frantic dance. Her hands found purchase on his shoulders, then tangled in his hair, pulling him closer until there was no space left between them.

Devon's lips trailed from her mouth, down her jaw, to the sensitive skin of her neck. His teeth grazed the delicate flesh there, not enough to break skin but enough to send shivers cascading down her spine. Kate's head fell back instinctively, exposing more of her throat to his ministrations, a soft whimper escaping her lips at the exquisite sensation.

His mouth moved lower, pressing reverent kisses to her collarbone, then down to the swell of her breasts. Kate's breath caught as his lips closed around one sensitive peak, his tongue circling the stiff nipple before his teeth grazed it gently. Her back arched off the bed, pressing herself more firmly against his mouth, her hands tangling in his dark hair.

"Devon," she breathed, his name a prayer on her lips as he worshiped her breasts, alternating between gentle suction and the careful scrape of his teeth. When he moved to her other breast, Kate's fingers tightened in his hair, holding him to her as waves of sensation crashed over her.

His hand moved from her waist, sliding down her hip to between her thighs. Kate's shuddered as his fingers found her center, stroking, teasing, igniting a fire that spread rapidly through her veins. Her hips instinctively lifted, pressing into his hand, a desperate, primal urge for friction, for release. Devon's mouth continued exploring her body, kissing the sensitive skin of her ribs, her stomach, her hip bones. Kate's body trembled beneath his work, logical thought seeping out her mind.

He watched her, his gaze never leaving hers, as his fingers crafted their magic, each stroke deepening the exquisite torment. Kate's own hands grew bolder, exploring the planes of his chest, the defined muscles of his abdomen. When her fingers wrapped around his cock, Devon groaned, his head falling forward in surrender as she stroked him with tentative touches that grew more confident with each passing moment.

He leaned down, his lips brushing hers, then whispered against her mouth, "I am yours, Kate, if you will have me."

Kate responded with a desperate, wordless plea. Her body undulated beneath him, her legs parting wider to invite him in. Devon positioned himself between her thighs. Kate felt the pressure of him against her and gasped. He shuddered as he entered her slowly, deliberately, watching her eyes, witnessing every sensation that crossed her face. Kate cried out, a muffled gasp of pure pleasure, her body stretching to accommodate him, welcoming him home.

As he began to move within her, Devon's hand found hers, their fingers intertwining as he established a slow, powerful rhythm. The simple connection of their joined hands somehow made the intimacy even more profound, an anchor point of tenderness midst the growing passion. Kate's free hand tangled in his hair, pulling his head down so she could press her lips to his neck, her teeth grazing the sensitive skin there just as he had done to her. Devon groaned at the sensation, his rhythm faltering for a moment before he regained control.

His slow, powerful rhythm drove deep into her and Kate's body responded instinctively in an uninhibited dance. Her head fell back, throat exposed, and Devon's fangs grazed her neck again, a soft, tantalizing pressure that sent shivers down her spine. Her body shook with the exquisite sensation and sinful pleasure of his touch.

They moved as one, a hungry dance of bodies entwined, each seeking to consume the other and lose themselves in the overwhelming tide of sensation. The chamber, once a place of punishment, was now a crucible of passion. Their cries were swallowed by the thick air, but their bodies spoke a language of raw, uninhibited desire. The undeniable truth that, despite everything, they were absolutely screaming for this, for each other, for release.

When the climax finally broke over them, it was a shattering, all-consuming wave which left them breathless, trembling, and entwined. Devon's hand still held hers as they rode out the aftershocks together. He rolled over and Kate collapsed against him, her heart pounding against his chest. He held her close, his own body still thrumming with the aftershocks of their intimacy.

They lay entangled in silence, the chamber now filled with the soft sounds of their recovery and the lingering scent of their passion. This was not just physical release; it was a communion, a silent conversation of souls, a desperate need finally fulfilled.

In that shared silence, in the aftermath of their wordless intimacy, Kate knew that she was utterly and completely his. Not as a captive, but as a woman who had chosen her path with open eyes and an open heart.

Chapter 12

Kate woke up in an unfamiliar place. The soft morning light came through the thin curtains, making her feel momentarily disoriented. This wasn't her suite. It wasn't the room where she had spent the night with Devon.

Memory returned in gentle waves of Devon, carrying her from the chamber after she had fallen asleep in his arms, bringing her to his personal quarters rather than returning her to her own suite. Kate sat up slowly, drawing the silk sheets around her. Devon was nowhere to be seen, but a note rested on the pillow beside her, written in elegant script:

> *Kate,*
>
> *Daylight is responsible for my absence, otherwise I would never have left your side. Please consider these rooms yours to use as you wish. Marcus will attend to any needs you may have.*
>
> *Until evening, D.*

Devon was offering her access to his most private space, a gesture of trust that spoke volumes after their night together. Kate rose from the bed, wrapping herself in a midnight blue silk robe that had been left for her. She moved through the suite with curiosity, taking in details she hadn't noticed during her brief time here before: The carefully curated art on the walls, the antique desk with documents neatly arranged, the bookshelves filled with volumes in multiple languages spanning centuries.

This was Devon's space where he retreated from the world. And he had invited her into it, not as a captive or guest, but as… what exactly? Partner? Lover? The terms felt both inadequate and presumptuous after just one night together, despite the intensity of their connection.

A knock at the door interrupted her thoughts.

"Ms Morgan?" Marcus's voice called. "I've brought breakfast, if you're awake."

Kate tightened the robe around herself. "Come in, Marcus."

The door opened to reveal Devon's assistant carrying a tray with coffee, fresh fruit, and pastries. His expression betrayed no surprise or judgment at finding Kate in his employer's quarters, his professional demeanor firmly in place.

"Good morning," he said, setting the tray on a small table near the window. "Mr Karlov asked that I ensure you have everything you need today."

"Thank you," Kate replied, suddenly aware of the awkwardness of the situation. What did one say to the assistant of the vampire with whom one had just spent the night?

Marcus seemed to sense her discomfort. "Mr Karlov also asked me to inform you that you have full access to the estate and grounds. The car and driver are at your disposal should you wish to go into Budapest or elsewhere."

The message was clear: Devon was making good on his promise of freedom, ensuring Kate understood she was not confined to the estate despite their new intimacy.

"There's one more thing," Marcus added, his tone shifting slightly. "Mr Karlov received an invitation this morning that he wished me to discuss with you."

Kate's curiosity was piqued. "An invitation?"

"To the Midwinter Conclave," Marcus explained. "A significant gathering in Mr Karlov's… community. It takes place three nights from now."

Something in Marcus's tone suggested this was more than a simple social engagement.

"His community?" Kate prompted. "You mean other vampires?"

Marcus nodded, his expression carefully neutral. "Yes. The Conclave happens twice yearly, at midwinter and midsummer. It's an important occasion for maintaining alliances and addressing matters of mutual concern."

Kate took a seat at the table, gesturing for Marcus to continue as she poured herself coffee. "And Devon wants me to attend with him?"

"He wished me to explain certain aspects of the Conclave to you," Marcus replied diplomatically.

"So that you might make an informed decision about whether to accompany him."

The careful phrasing caught Kate's attention. "What aspects?"

Marcus hesitated, choosing his words with evident care. "The vampires who attend these gatherings often bring human companions. These companions serve various roles within vampire society, some as advisors, others as artists or scholars under patronage, and some…" he paused, "as what are traditionally called 'Pet'"

The term sent an immediate chill through Kate. "Pet," she repeated flatly.

"It's a fairly modern practice," Marcus explained quickly. "A formalized relationship between vampire and human with mutual benefits. The human receives protection and financial security. In return, they provide… services to their patron."

"They're blood banks," Kate translated bluntly.

"Not quite so simple," Marcus countered. "Many such relationships are quite complex, with genuine affection and respect on both sides. Some Pets serve their patrons for decades, becoming trusted companions and confidants."

Kate set down her coffee cup with deliberate care. "And how will I know who is Pet and vampire at these gatherings?"

Here, Marcus's discomfort increased visibly. "Pets usually wear formal collars during ceremonial events, often quite beautiful and ornate. Many also bear a mark, a tattoo or brand that identifies their patron's house."

"A brand," Kate said, her voice hardening. "Like livestock."

"The marking is consensual; many Pets view it with pride, as a symbol of belonging to a powerful house. The relationship provides them with access to vampire society, protection from other supernatural threats, and often considerable wealth and influence."

Kate rose from the table, moving to the window to look out at the sunlit gardens below. The contrast between the beauty of the morning and the derogatory practice being described was jarring.

"And Devon expects me to attend this Conclave as his 'Pet'?" she asked, her back still to Marcus.

"Mr Karlov made it clear that he wishes you to attend as his companion," Marcus corrected carefully. "However, he also wished you to understand the social context and expectations. At such gatherings, unmarked humans are typically viewed as… unaffiliated. Unprotected."

The implication was clear, without some visible sign of Devon's claim, Kate would be considered available by other vampires at the gathering.

"So my choices are to wear a collar and pretend to be property, or risk becoming actual prey," Kate summarized, turning back to face Marcus.

"Mr Karlov is exploring alternatives," Marcus assured her. "He has no desire to place you in an uncomfortable position. That's why he wanted you to have this information now, so you might discuss options with him this evening."

Kate nodded slowly, processing the information. "Tell me more about this Conclave. Who attends? What actually happens there?"

Marcus looked relieved to be on safer ground. "The Conclave serves several purposes. It's a social gathering and a political assembly. Representatives from major vampire houses across Europe attend, along with some from other regions. They discuss territorial disputes, trade agreements, responses to threats from other supernatural communities, and legal issues within vampire society."

"Vampire law?" Kate asked, curious even though she felt uneasy about the Pet system.

"Oh yes," Marcus replied. "Vampire society is very organized, with old laws addressing everything from territorial rights to making new vampires. The Conclave serves as both a legislature and a court for matters that impact several houses or regions."

This was a side of vampire society Kate hadn't considered, not just predators hiding in the shadows, but an organized civilization with its own governance and politics.

"And Devon's role in all this?" she pressed.

"Mr Karlov represents one of the older houses, his lineage traces back over centuries. This grants him considerable influence. He's often called upon to mediate disputes or provide counsel on matters."

Kate absorbed this information, beginning to understand that Devon's world was far more complex than she had imagined. "What kind of disputes?"

"Territorial conflicts, usually. Disagreements over feeding rights in major cities, or responses to human authorities who become too curious about vampire activities. Sometimes matters of succession when a house leader passes or steps down."

Kate found herself fascinated despite her concerns about the Pet system. This was an entire hidden world operating alongside human society, with its own politics, conflicts, and alliances.

"Thank you for your honesty, Marcus," she said finally. "I'd like to go into Budapest today. There are some things I need to think about, and I do my best thinking away from… all this."

If Marcus was surprised by her request, he didn't show it. "I'll arrange for the car. What time would you like to leave?"

"In an hour," Kate decided. "And Marcus? I'd prefer to go alone. Just the driver, no security detail."

Now, concern flickered across his features. "Ms Morgan, Mr Karlov would be concerned for your safety if—"

"I'm not a prisoner anymore, Marcus," Kate interrupted gently. "Devon promised me freedom to come and go as I choose. I'm choosing to go into the city alone today."

Marcus studied her for a long moment, then nodded. "Very well. I'll inform the driver. He'll be ready in an hour."

After he left, Kate went back to the window, her thoughts scattered. The Pet system troubled her deeply. It threatened the peace she had found with Devon's nature and their changing relationship. Was this what lay ahead for her as Devon's companion? A collar around her neck, a brand on her skin, being shown off to his kind as a possession rather than a partner? The thought was at odds with everything she had come to believe about their connection.

And yet, she couldn't dismiss Marcus's explanation entirely. If such gatherings were an important part of Devon's world, his society, could she simply refuse to participate? Would that force him to choose between his place in vampire society and his relationship with her?

* * *

Budapest was glorious as it unfolded around Kate in a dream of normalcy. It seemed like forever since Kate had last led a simple, normal, human day. The driver had dropped her at the Castle District as requested, with instructions to return for her in four hours.

Four hours of freedom, of anonymity, of being just another tourist in a beautiful European city. Kate walked the cobblestone streets with deliberate slowness, taking in the architecture, the sounds, the scents of a world that had seemed increasingly distant during her time at Devon's estate.

She visited shops and spoke with shopkeepers and café owners in halting phrases from the Hungarian phrasebook she had studied during her captivity. The normality of these interactions was both comforting and disorienting after the extraordinary developments of recent days.

In a small boutique near Fisherman's Bastion, Kate found herself examining elegant evening gowns, her mind turning inevitably to the Conclave Marcus had described. If she chose to attend with Devon, she would need appropriate attire, something that reflected her status not as a Pet but as a partner, an equal.

"Special occasion?" the shopkeeper asked in accented English, noting Kate's interest in a particularly striking gown of emerald green silk.

"A formal event," Kate replied vaguely. "Something… complicated."

The woman smiled knowingly. "Meeting the family? Always complicated."

Kate couldn't help but laugh at the unintentional accuracy of the assessment. "Something like that."

She left the boutique without purchasing anything, her thoughts still too unsettled to make such a decision. Instead, she found herself drawn to a small art supply store tucked away on a side street. She purchased a small sketchbook with a set of charcoal pencils, and made her way to a quiet café overlooking the Danube. Kate began to sketch as she sipped espresso. Not the cityscape before her, but images from her mind's eye. Devon's face in repose during dormancy. The chamber that had been her prison and become their sanctuary. The estate seen from the gardens at night.

It was her way of processing her experiences and emotions, art had always been her refuge. Turning to a fresh page, Kate found herself drawing something unexpected, a self-portrait, her neck adorned with a collar. The image gave her the chills, but she didn't stop, adding details that emerged from her imagination.

But what if? She turned to a new page, and in this sketch she placed herself at Devon's side, without a collar or mark, standing as an equal rather than a possession. They were surrounded by vampiric figures who regarded this anomaly with expressions ranging from curiosity to hostility.

Was this what awaited them if she attended the Conclave as Devon's companion rather than his Pet? Social censure and possibly danger. Kate closed the sketchbook. She had made her decision. She would attend the Conclave on her own terms, not as a Pet or as property. They would have to face the consequences of this choice together. It was a test to see if their connection could survive the pressures of Devon's world.

Kate spent her remaining time in the city more purposefully, returning to the boutique to purchase the emerald green gown and other items she would need for the Conclave. By the time the driver returned to collect her, she felt centered in a way she hadn't since learning about the gathering that morning.

The drive back to the estate passed in contemplative silence, Kate watching the city give way to countryside, then to the familiar winding road that led to what she now thought of, with some surprise, as home. Not a prison anymore, not merely a residence, but a place where she had chosen to be, where someone awaited her return.

As the car passed through the main gates, Kate noted that twilight was approaching, Devon would be awakening soon, if he hadn't already. Their conversation tonight would be challenging, perhaps even painful, but necessary if they were to move forward together. Marcus met her at the entrance, taking the packages from the driver with his usual efficiency.

"Mr Karlov is in the music room," he informed her. "He asked to be notified when you returned."

"Thank you, Marcus," Kate replied. "Please tell him I'll join him shortly. I'd like to freshen up first."

In her suite Kate took her time preparing to face the conversation ahead. She showered, changed into a simple yet elegant dress, and carefully arranged her purchases in the closet. The emerald green gown she hung prominently, a visual reminder of her decision.

When she finally made her way to the music room, Kate paused in the doorway, taking a moment to observe Devon unnoticed. He sat at the grand piano, playing a piece she recognized as Debussy's "Clair de Lune," his expression one of complete absorption in the music. In this moment, he appeared human, an artist lost in his craft. It was this Devon she had connected with, this Devon she had chosen despite what he was and their complicated beginning. Could this Devon exist alongside the vampire who moved in a society that viewed humans as possessions?

Sensing her presence, Devon looked up from the piano, his fingers stilling on the keys. "Kate," he said simply, his eyes taking in her appearance with evident appreciation.

"Don't stop," she said, moving into the room. "It's beautiful."

Devon continued to play, the delicate notes filling the space between them as Kate took a seat near the piano. She watched his hands move across the keys, remembering how those same hands had touched her with such care the night before.

When the piece finished, Devon turned to face her fully, his expression serious. "Marcus told me about your conversation this morning."

"About the Conclave," Kate confirmed. "About the Pet system and collars and marks."

Devon nodded, his eyes never leaving hers. "I should have discussed it with you myself. I apologize for delegating such a sensitive matter."

"I've made my decision," she said, meeting Devon's gaze steadily. "I'll attend the Conclave with you."

Relief flickered across Devon's features, quickly replaced by caution. "There are complications we need to discuss," he said. "Expectations and traditions that—"

"I won't be your Pet," Kate interrupted firmly. "I won't wear a collar or bear a mark. If I attend, it will be as your partner, your equal."

Devon was silent for a long moment, studying her with those ancient eyes that had seen centuries pass. "That would be… unprecedented," he said finally. "In our society, humans are not acknowledged as equals, particularly not at formal gatherings like the Conclave."

"Then perhaps it's time for that to change," Kate replied. "Or at least, for you to take a stand for what you believe."

"And what do I believe, Kate?" Devon asked softly.

"That's what I need to know," she said. "Last night, in the chamber, what happened between us wasn't the connection between master and Pet. It was something deeper, something equal despite our different natures. Am I wrong?"

Devon rose from the piano bench, moving to stand before her. "No," he said with quiet intensity. "You're not wrong. What we shared was genuine, equal in the ways that matter most."

"Then how can you participate in a society that views humans as possessions?" Kate pressed. "How can you ask me to enter that world, even peripherally?"

Devon sighed, a sound that seemed to carry the weight of centuries. "My world is ancient, Kate, with traditions and hierarchies established over millennia. Change comes slowly, when it comes at all."

"That doesn't answer my question," Kate persisted.

Devon was silent for a moment, considering his words carefully. "I have existed within this society for centuries," he said finally. "Accepting its structures and traditions as the price of belonging, of having a place among my kind. Until you, I never had reason to question those traditions deeply."

"And now?" Kate prompted.

"Now I find myself at a crossroads," Devon admitted. "Between the world I have known for centuries and the possibility you represent, a connection that defies the traditional boundaries between our kinds."

Kate stood, bringing herself to eye level with Devon. "I won't be your Pet," she said simply. "Not for one night, not for appearance's sake, not to satisfy the expectations of your society. If that means I can't attend the Conclave, or that attending would place us both in a difficult position, then we need to consider whether this relationship can work at all."

The ultimatum hung in the air between them, not delivered as a threat but as a simple statement of fact. Kate watched emotions play across Devon's features, conflict, concern, and something deeper that might have been admiration.

"There may be a third option," he said finally. "Not traditional, not without risk, but perhaps a way forward that honors both your autonomy and the reality of my world."

"I'm listening," Kate said, cautious but open.

"You could attend not as my Pet, but as my protégée," Devon suggested. "A human artist under my patronage, being introduced to society as someone of special talent and interest. It would be unusual but not unprecedented. Several of the older vampires have taken human protégés over the centuries, artists, musicians, scholars of exceptional ability."

Kate considered the suggestion, turning it over in her mind. "And this would exempt me from the… expectations placed on the Pet?"

"Largely, yes," Devon confirmed. "You would not be required to wear a collar or bear a mark. You would be introduced by name and profession, acknowledged as an individual rather than a possession."

"But?" Kate prompted, sensing there was more.

"But it would still place you in a subordinate position," Devon acknowledged. "Not as property, but as student to master, recipient of patronage. And it would not fully protect you from the interest or advances of others at the Conclave."

"How would you protect me, then?" Kate asked.

"With my presence, my reputation, and if necessary, my power," Devon replied simply. "My house is one of the oldest, my lineage respected. Few would risk my displeasure by showing disrespect to someone under my protection."

Kate nodded slowly, processing the information. "And our personal relationship? Would that be acknowledged, or hidden?"

Devon hesitated, and in that hesitation, Kate found her answer. "Hidden," she concluded. "At least publicly."

"For your protection," Devon explained. "A romantic connection between vampire and human is not forbidden, exactly, but it is unusual. Viewed with suspicion or derision by many."

"So I would pretend to be merely your artistic project," Kate said, testing the idea aloud. "While privately being your lover."

"For this Conclave, yes," Devon confirmed. "As we navigate the complexities of introducing you to my world. In time, perhaps things could be different."

Kate turned away, moving to the window to look out at the darkening gardens. The compromise Devon offered was not ideal, it still required an act, still placed her in a position of lesser status in the eyes of his society. But it avoided the degrading nature of the Pet system while acknowledging the reality of the world they must navigate together.

Kate turned back to face him, her decision made. "I'll attend as your protégée," she said. "But I want something in return."

Devon's eyebrow raised slightly. "What would that be?"

"Honesty," Kate replied simply. "About your world, your society. If we're to have any chance of building something real between us, I need to understand everything, not just the parts you choose to show me."

Devon was silent for a long moment, weighing her request. Then he nodded, a gesture of acceptance and perhaps respect. "Agreed," he said. "Beginning now, if you wish."

* * *

Two nights before the Conclave, Devon received an unexpected visitor. Kate was in her studio, working on a new painting inspired by her recent experiences, when Marcus appeared at the door with an expression of barely concealed concern.

"Ms Morgan," he said with his usual formality. "Mr Karlov requests your presence in the main salon. He has a guest he wishes you to meet."

Kate set down her brushes, curiosity piqued. Devon had mentioned no expected visitors, and since her arrival at the estate, there had been none save for staff and delivery personnel. "Who is it?" she asked, wiping paint from her hands.

"Lord Aleksander Voss," Marcus replied, his tone carefully neutral though something in his expression suggested caution. "A… significant figure in vampire society."

The hesitation was subtle but noticeable. "Not a friend?" Kate pressed.

"Lord Voss represents one of the most powerful houses in Eastern Europe," Marcus said diplomatically. "His family and Mr Karlov's have… a complex history spanning several centuries."

The non-answer was answer enough. Kate nodded, taking a moment to change from her paint-spattered shirt into something more presentable before following Marcus to the main salon.

The room was one Kate had seen only rarely during her time at the estate, a formal space used for receiving guests rather than daily living. Its high ceilings and elegant furnishings spoke of old wealth and refined taste, with artwork and artifacts that spanned centuries of collection.

Devon stood near the fireplace, engaged in conversation with a man Kate had never seen before. He was tall, lean with sharp features and blonde hair styled in an artfully tousled manner. His suit was impeccably tailored, modern in cut but with subtle details that hinted at older fashion sensibilities. There was something about his casual confidence that bordered on arrogance that immediately put Kate on guard.

As Kate entered, both men turned toward her. Devon's expression was composed but watchful, while the stranger, Aleksander Voss, regarded her with undisguised interest and assessment.

Devon extended a hand toward Kate in invitation. "Aleksander, may I present Katherine Morgan, the artist I mentioned. Kate, this is Lord Aleksander Voss, an old acquaintance."

Kate moved forward to join them, noting the careful phrasing of Devon's introduction. Not friend or colleague, but acquaintance a neutral term that revealed little about their actual relationship.

"Ms Morgan," Aleksander said, taking her offered hand and bringing it to his lips in an old-world gesture that seemed practiced rather than sincere. His touch was cold, and Kate suppressed a shiver as his pale green eyes studied her with calculating intensity. "Devon has been quite secretive about you. I had to come see for myself what has kept him so preoccupied these past months."

Kate felt as if she were being catalogued, her value calculated in some internal ledger. "Lord Voss," she acknowledged, gently but firmly reclaiming her hand. "I wasn't aware that Devon had mentioned me to his acquaintances."

"Not directly, no," Aleksander replied with a cold smile. "But one hears things, even about someone as private as our Devon. A New York artist, brought to Budapest for a special exhibition, then mysteriously extending her stay for months? It caught my curiosity."

It was clear that Aleksander had been keeping tabs on Devon, aware of Kate's presence long before this visit. The realization sent a chill through her, but she kept herself composed.

"My work has benefited greatly from the change of scenery," she said simply. "Devon has been a generous patron."

"Patron," Aleksander repeated, the word carrying a weight of innuendo. "How very Renaissance of him. Though I don't recall the Medicis keeping their artists quite so close, or for quite so long."

Devon's expression remained neutral, but Kate sensed a tension in his posture that hadn't been there moments before. "Kate's talent deserves nurturing," he said smoothly. "Her work has evolved remarkably during her time here."

"I look forward to seeing it at the Conclave," Aleksander replied, his gaze still fixed on Kate. "Devon tells me you'll be attending as his protégée. Quite an honor for a human artist, to be introduced to our society."

The emphasis he placed on "human" was subtle but unmistakable, a reminder of the fundamental difference between Kate and the company she would be keeping at the Conclave.

"I consider myself fortunate," Kate replied, matching his tone of polite insincerity. "Though I admit to some nervousness about the event. I understand the Conclave has certain traditions that might be unfamiliar to an outsider."

Aleksander's smile widened slightly, something predatory entering his expression. "Indeed it does. Though I'm sure Devon has prepared you adequately. He's always been so considerate of his human companions."

The barb was thinly veiled, suggesting a history Kate wasn't privy to. She glanced at Devon, noting the slight tightening around his eyes, the only visible sign that Aleksander's comment had struck a nerve.

"Perhaps we should move to the drawing room," Devon suggested smoothly. "Marcus has prepared refreshments.

As they relocated to the more intimate setting of the drawing room, Kate observed the dynamic between the two vampires with growing interest and concern. There was history here, and tension that went beyond mere acquaintanceship. Aleksander moved with a casual confidence that bordered on presumption, examining objects and artwork as if assessing their value rather than appreciating their beauty.

"You've acquired new pieces since my last visit," he commented, pausing before a small sculpture Kate recognized as a rare Giacometti. "Your taste remains impeccable, if expensive."

"Art is the one extravagance that consistently rewards the investment," Devon replied. "Both financially and spiritually."

"Speaking of investments," Aleksander said, turning his attention back to Kate as they settled into their seats, "I'm curious about your work, Ms Morgan. What medium do you prefer?"

Kate sensed an underlying motive beyond mere curiosity. Nevertheless, she answered honestly, describing her mixed media approach. Aleksander listened, asking follow-up questions suggested a knowledge of contemporary art. Kate began to relax slightly, wondering if maybe she had misread him.

"Will Gerald be accompanying you to the Conclave?" Devon asked suddenly, his tone casual but his eyes watchful. "I haven't seen him in some time."

Something flickered across Aleksander's features, too quick for Kate to interpret, but Devon's slight tension suggested he had caught it.

"Ah, Gerald," Aleksander said with a dismissive wave of his hand. "No, I'm afraid Gerald won't be attending. He proved to be less adaptable than I had hoped. You know how it is with Pets, sometimes they simply lose their charm."

The casual cruelty in his tone made Kate's stomach turn, though she kept her expression carefully neutral. There was something in the way he spoke of Gerald, as if discussing a broken toy rather than a person.

"A pity," Devon said, sounding casual, but Kate noted the slight tension in his voice. "He seemed devoted to you."

"I prefer companions who can grow with my interests," Aleksander replied with a shrug. He glanced meaningfully at Kate. "Though I find myself increasingly drawn to artistic personalities. There's something fascinating about the creative mind, don't you think? It processes experiences and turns complex emotions into something real."

Kate felt a chill at the predatory interest in his voice, the way his eyes assessed her as if she were a particularly intriguing specimen. Devon's hand moved almost imperceptibly closer to hers on the arm of his chair, a subtle gesture of protection and possession.

"Artists do tend to have unique perspectives," Devon agreed carefully. "Though they also tend to be quite independent in their thinking. Not everyone appreciates that quality."

"Oh, but I do," Aleksander said, his smile sharp. "Independence can be so much more rewarding to cultivate. The process of helping someone discover new aspects of themselves, new depths of feeling and expression. It's an art form in itself."

The conversation had taken on an undercurrent that made Kate's skin crawl. She was beginning to understand what had happened to Gerald, and what Aleksander was implying about his interest in her. As Marcus served their drinks Aleksander shifted the conversation abruptly.

"Tell me, Ms Morgan, how are you finding life at Devon's estate? It must be quite an adjustment from New York City."

"It's been a productive environment for my work," Kate replied carefully.

"And socially?" Aleksander pressed. "Devon keeps a rather… isolated household. Don't you find it limiting? A vibrant young woman like yourself must crave more diverse company occasionally."

Before Kate could respond, Devon interjected smoothly. "Kate has full access to Budapest whenever she wishes. She's hardly isolated here."

"Of course," Aleksander conceded with a smile that suggested he didn't believe it for a moment.

"Still, there's a difference between visiting a city as a tourist and truly engaging with its society. Perhaps after the Conclave, you might allow me to introduce Ms Morgan to some of Budapest's more… exclusive artistic circles? I maintain connections with several galleries and collectors who would be fascinated by her work."

Kate didn't miss the challenge underlying the generous offer, Aleksander was testing boundaries, seeing how Devon would respond to his interest in Kate.

"That's very kind," Kate replied before Devon could speak, maintaining her agency in the conversation. "Though my schedule is quite full at present with preparations for several new pieces."

"Another time, perhaps," Aleksander said, his eyes moving between Kate and Devon with calculating interest. "The offer remains open"

The conversation continued in this vein for another hour, pleasant on the surface, but charged with undercurrents of challenge and assessment. Aleksander probed delicately but persistently for details about Kate's relationship with Devon, while Devon maintained a careful balance between hospitality and reserve.

When Aleksander finally rose to leave, Kate felt as if she had endured a subtle but exhausting interrogation. At the door, the visitor took her hand once more, holding it slightly longer than propriety demanded.

"Until the Conclave, Ms Morgan," he said, his voice lowered for her ears alone. "I look forward to continuing our conversation in a more… stimulating environment."

After Marcus had escorted Aleksander out, Kate turned to Devon, who stood watching the departing car with an expression that mingled concern and irritation.

"That wasn't a social call, was it?" she asked directly.

Devon shook his head slightly. "No. Aleksander rarely does anything without multiple purposes."

"What does he want?" Kate pressed.

Devon was silent for a moment, considering his response. "Information, primarily. About you, about your place here, about how your presence might affect the balance of power within our society."

"It felt more personal than political curiosity," Kate observed. "There's history between you two."

Devon turned to face her fully, his expression serious. "Yes. Old wounds and a complicated history that spans centuries. Aleksander and I have known each other since before the French Revolution. We've been allies at times, rivals at others."

"And now?" Kate asked.

"Now we maintain a careful equilibrium. Our houses have too much shared history for open hostility, but too many fundamental disagreements for genuine friendship."

"Is he dangerous?" Kate asked directly.

Devon considered the question with evident care. "Not in the direct, physical sense he wouldn't risk open aggression against someone under my protection. But in other ways… yes. Aleksander is dangerous in his ambition, his calculation, his willingness to exploit any perceived weakness or opportunity."

"And I'm a perceived weakness," Kate concluded.

"Or an opportunity," Devon corrected. "Depending on his assessment of our relationship and how it might be leveraged to his advantage."

Kate absorbed this information, connecting it to the undercurrents she had sensed during their interaction with Aleksander. "He'll be at the Conclave."

"Yes," Devon confirmed. "Along with many others who will be curious about you, about us. The protégée story will satisfy some, but not all, particularly not Aleksander, who knows me too well to accept such a simple explanation."

"Then we need to be prepared," Kate said decisively. "I need to understand exactly what we're walking into, and how to navigate it without creating problems for either of us."

Devon's expression softened a bit, showing a mix of pride and concern in his eyes. "Yes," he said. "We do."

The Conclave would test their relationship and Kate's skill in handling a society based on power dynamics that she was just starting to grasp. Aleksander Voss would be lurking at the edges of this test, watching and looking for any chance to use the situation to his benefit.

Chapter 13

The night before the Midwinter Gathering brought an unexpected snowfall. Kate stood at the window of her studio, watching the large flakes drift lazily through the darkness, illuminated by the soft glow of exterior lights.

Her conversations with Devon about vampire society had left her unsettled, despite their compromise of the protégée arrangement. And Aleksander's visit had only heightened her anxiety, introducing an element of danger and calculation to what was already a complex situation.

Kate turned back to her canvas, where she had been attempting to capture her conflicted emotions through abstract forms and colors. The painting was chaotic, all sharp angles and clashing hues, a visual representation of her internal state that satisfied her artistic sensibilities but did little to calm her mind.

She was so absorbed in her work that she didn't hear Devon enter until he spoke from the doorway.

"Your technique has evolved," he observed quietly. "There's a boldness here I haven't seen before."

Kate glanced over her shoulder, brush in hand. Devon stood watching her with genuine interest, dressed in dark trousers and a simple blue sweater that made him look irresistible.

"It's how I process," she explained, turning back to the canvas. "When words fail, colors and shapes can express what I'm feeling."

Devon moved closer, studying the painting with the careful attention he brought to all art. "And what are you feeling?" he asked.

Kate considered the question, adding another stroke of deep crimson to the canvas before answering. "Conflicted. Anxious. About tomorrow night, what it represents."

"The gathering," Devon nodded in understanding.

"Not just the gathering," Kate clarified, setting down her brush and turning to face him fully. "Everything it represents, your world, its traditions, the place of humans within it. The way it conflicts with what's happening between us."

Devon was silent for a moment, his ancient eyes thoughtful as they moved from the painting back to Kate's face. "Would you walk with me?" he asked finally. "There's something I'd like to show you."

Curiosity piqued, Kate nodded, cleaning her brushes quickly before following Devon from the studio. Instead of leading her toward the main house, he guided her down a corridor she had never explored, then down a spiral staircase that descended deeper than she had realized the estate extended.

At the bottom of the staircase, they reached a wooden door reinforced with iron bands. Devon produced an old-fashioned key from his pocket, turning it in the lock with a sound that suggested the mechanism was well-maintained despite its apparent age.

The door swung open to reveal a large chamber illuminated by soft, indirect lighting. The room was a gallery unlike any Kate had ever seen. Artwork from across centuries lined the walls and filled carefully arranged display cases.

"What is this place?" she asked, her voice hushed with wonder as she stepped inside.

"My personal collection," Devon replied, closing the door behind them. "Gathered over centuries, preserved here where light and time can do minimal damage."

Kate moved slowly through the space, overwhelmed by the breadth and quality of the collection. Here was a small Rembrandt sketch, there a Rodin Marquette, beside it what appeared to be an ancient Egyptian papyrus. The collection spanned cultures, periods, and mediums with a breadth that spoke of centuries of careful acquisition.

"These should be in museums," she murmured, pausing before a small painting she recognized as an early Matisse.

"Some were, at various points," Devon acknowledged. "Others came to me directly from the artists themselves."

Kate turned to him, a new understanding dawning. "You knew them. The artists."

Devon nodded, melancholy touching his features. "Many of them, yes. Some as friends, some as…" he hesitated, then continued, "some as companions."

The meaning was clear, Devon had had relationships with humans before, perhaps many times over his long existence. The realization shouldn't have surprised Kate, given his age, but it affected her nonetheless.

"Were they your Pets?" she asked directly, needing to understand.

Devon's expression grew serious. "No," he said firmly. "Never that. The Pet system is relatively modern In earlier centuries, vampires and humans who chose to associate did so without such rigid structures."

"Then why accept it now?" Kate pressed. "Why participate in a system you clearly find distasteful?"

Devon moved to a nearby bench, gesturing for Kate to join him. When she did, he continued, his voice thoughtful.

"Immortality brings a certain inertia," he explained. "When you've existed for centuries, change becomes both constant and distant something that happens around you rather than to you. You observe it, adapt to it superficially, but your core remains anchored in earlier times, earlier values."

"That sounds like an excuse," Kate observed gently.

"Perhaps it is," Devon acknowledged. "The truth is more complex, and less flattering to my kind. While human society evolved toward equality rights, vampire society remained hierarchical and traditional. The Pet system came about as a compromise between our need for human blood and the changing human world around us, to provide structure and rules."

"Rules that still treat humans as lesser beings," Kate pointed out.

"Yes," Devon agreed simply. "A reflection of the fundamental power imbalance between our kinds."

They sat in silence for a moment, the weight of centuries and cultural differences hanging between them. Then Devon rose and offered his hand to Kate.

"Come," he said. "There's more I want to show you."

He led her deeper into the gallery, past displays of increasingly ancient artifacts, to a section that appeared more personal in nature. Here were smaller items, letters, sketches, photographs, and mementos arranged with evident care.

"These," Devon said softly, "are remembrances of the humans who have mattered to me over the centuries. Not possessions or Pets, but individuals who touched my existence in meaningful ways."

Kate examined the display with growing wonder. There were daguerreotypes from the early days of photography, sketches that appeared to date from the Renaissance, letters written in faded ink on yellowed paper. Each item was labeled with a name and date, some spanning only a few years, others decades.

"You cared for them," Kate said, not a question but a realization.

"Yes," Devon confirmed. "Each in different ways, each leaving their mark on me despite the brevity of their lives compared to mine."

Kate's fingers hovered over a small watercolor sketch of a garden, dated 1789. "What happened to them? To all of them?"

Devon's expression held centuries of accumulated loss. "What happens to all humans, eventually. They aged. They died. I remained."

The simple statement contained volumes of grief and loneliness that Kate could only begin to comprehend. To care for someone, knowing from the beginning that you would outlive them by centuries, the courage such connections required suddenly struck her with full force.

"Is that why you abducted me?" she asked quietly. "Because you couldn't bear to watch another human you cared for age and die?"

Devon was silent for a long moment, considering her question with the careful thought he brought to all serious matters. "No," he said finally. "That was never my conscious motivation, perhaps unconsciously… But no, my reasons were both simpler and more complex. I saw in you a kindred spirit, someone who understood isolation and longing as I did. I wanted to possess that understanding, to keep it close."

"Like these," Kate gestured to the mementos around them.

"Yes," Devon acknowledged. "Though I came to realize that possessing the art was not the same as connecting with the artist. That keeping you captive was not the same as truly knowing you."

Kate studied his face, seeing in it a vulnerability that his usual composed demeanor concealed. "And now?" she asked. "What do you want now?"

Devon turned to face her fully, his ancient eyes holding hers with an intensity that made her breath catch. "I want to know you," he said simply. "Not possess you, not keep you as a beautiful object in my collection, but truly know you. Your thoughts, your dreams, your fears. I want to be known by you in return."

Kate felt her heart race at the sincerity in his voice, but a darker thought crept in as she looked around at all the mementos of his past relationships. "And when you grow tired of me?" she asked quietly, her voice barely above a whisper. "When the novelty wears off, when you learn all there is to know about me? What happens when you decide you want something new, someone new?"

The question hung in the air between them, heavy with all of Kate's deepest fears about their impossible situation. She watched Devon's face carefully, looking for any flicker of uncertainty, any hint that her fears might be justified. Instead, she saw something that surprised her, pain. Deep, genuine pain at the thought that she might believe him capable of such casual dismissal.

"Kate," he said, his voice rough with emotion. He reached for her hands, holding them gently in his own. "Look around you. Do you see novelty here? Do you see the remnants of casual fascination?"

Kate glanced at the carefully preserved mementos, each one lovingly maintained, each representing decades of connection.

"These people," Devon continued, his thumb brushing across her knuckles, "I didn't tire of them. I didn't grow bored or seek something new. I loved them, each in their own way, and I mourned them when they were gone."

"But that's exactly what I mean," Kate said, her voice breaking slightly. "You've had centuries to perfect the art of loving and losing. What if I'm just another chapter in that long story? What if—"

"Stop," Devon said firmly, his hands moving to frame her face. "Kate, listen to me. I am introducing you to vampire society as my protégée. Do you understand what that means? What I'm risking?"

Kate shook her head, not trusting her voice.

"It means I'm publicly declaring my intentions toward you," Devon explained, his eyes never leaving hers. "I'm telling every vampire in our society that you are under my protection, that you matter to me, that any threat to you is a threat to me. I'm making myself vulnerable to political maneuvering, to challenges from those who would use you against me. I'm changing centuries of careful neutrality for you."

"Devon—"

"I'm not finished," he said gently but firmly. "I've lived for over four hundred years, Kate. In all that time, I have never introduced a human to vampire society in any capacity. Never. The risk was always too great. But with you..." He paused, his forehead coming to rest against hers. "With you, I find myself willing to risk everything."

Kate felt tears prick at her eyes. "But what if you change your mind? What if—"

"Then I would be a fool," Devon said simply. "Kate, I have spent centuries collecting beautiful things, preserving them, cherishing them. But you... you're not something to be collected. You're someone to be loved. And love, true love, doesn't fade with familiarity. It deepens."

He pulled back slightly to look into her eyes. "I cannot promise you immortality, that choice must be yours to make, if you ever choose to make it. But I can promise you this: For as long as you'll have me, for as long as your mortal life allows, you will be cherished. You will be protected. You will be loved with every fiber of my being."

Kate searched his face, seeing in it a sincerity that took her breath away. "You really mean that," she whispered.

"I have never meant anything more," Devon replied. "Tomorrow night, when I present you to vampire society, I'm not just introducing my protégée. I'm introducing the woman I love. The woman I choose, above all others, above all considerations of safety or tradition or political advantage."

Kate felt the last of her walls crumble at his words. She pressed onto her tiptoes to reach a hand around his head and bring his lips to meet hers in a soft kiss. "I love you too," she whispered, the admission feeling both terrifying and liberating.

Devon's eyes closed briefly, as if her words were a prayer answered. When he opened them again, they were bright with unshed tears. "Then trust me," he said. "Trust that what we have is worth the risks we're taking. Trust that my feelings for you aren't a passing fancy but something deeper than I've ever experienced."

Kate nodded, unable to speak past the emotion clogging her throat. In this underground chamber, surrounded by the remnants of Devon's past, she finally understood the magnitude of what he was offering her, his heart, his future, his very existence reshaped around loving her.

"I trust you," she managed to say, and meant it completely.

Here, surrounded by the evidence of centuries of existence, Devon was offering her a glimpse of his true self, not the cultured vampire aristocrat, not the powerful protector, but the being beneath those roles who had witnessed history unfold and carried the weight of that perspective through the centuries.

"Why show me this now?" Kate asked. "Why tonight?"

"Because tomorrow you enter my world more fully than before," Devon replied. "You'll see aspects of vampire society that are disturbing, ancient, contrary to your values and mine. I wanted you to understand that what exists between us exists in contrast to those traditions, not because of them."

Kate nodded slowly, absorbing the significance of what Devon was sharing. This underground gallery was more than a collection of art and mementos, it was a physical manifestation of his inner life, the parts of himself he kept hidden from the world above.

"Thank you," she said simply. "For trusting me with this."

Devon's expression softened, something like wonder crossing his features.

"It's strange," he said. "After centuries of existence, trust doesn't come easily to me. Yet with you…"

"With me?" Kate prompted when he didn't continue.

"With you, it feels natural," Devon finished. "Despite our beginning, despite the complications between us, trusting you feels like the path of least resistance rather than a conscious choice."

The admission hung in the air between them, profound in its simplicity. Kate moved closer to Devon, reaching out to take his hand in hers, a gesture that had become increasingly natural since their night in the chamber.

"Show me more," she said softly. "Show me the pieces that matter most to you."

For the next few hours, they walked through the gallery together. Devon shared stories about the artworks and the people linked to them. Kate listened and asked questions, captivated by this close look into his wide-ranging experience.

Their conversation flowed from the past to the present and toward their shared future. They talked about the gathering, Aleksander's clear interest, and the challenges they would face in navigating vampire society together.

"Are you sure you want to attend?" Devon asked as they finally headed back toward the entrance. "It would be okay to decide it's too soon or too complicated."

Kate considered the question seriously, weighing her anxiety against her determination. "I'm certain," she said finally. "Not because I'm eager to enter vampire society, but because I refuse to hide what's developing between us, even if we must present it differently to the world."

As they moved up the spiral staircase and left the underground gallery behind, Kate felt a change in her perspective. Whatever challenges awaited them tomorrow night, they would face them together with the foundation of trust that was deepening between them.

Devon paused at a window to watch the snowfall, gazing out at the transformed white landscape with evident appreciation.

"It's beautiful," Kate said, joining him at the window. "Like something from a fairy tale."

"Would you like to see it more closely?" Devon asked.

The invitation was unexpected, but welcome. Kate nodded, and Devon led her to a small side entrance where winter coats and boots were kept. As she bundled up against the cold, Kate was struck by the domesticity of the moment, so ordinary, so human.

Outside, the night was still and silent, the falling snow muffling all sound except the soft crunch of their footsteps. Devon guided Kate along paths he knew by heart, through gardens now transformed into sculptural landscapes of white. The cold air was invigorating, clearing Kate's mind of lingering anxiety and allowing her to simply be present in this moment of unexpected beauty.

They walked in comfortable silence for a time, then Devon spoke, his voice thoughtful in the quiet night.

"I've existed through countless winters," he said, "seen snow fall on these gardens more times than I can remember. Yet tonight, seeing it through your eyes, it feels new again."

Kate glanced at him, struck by the simple honesty of the observation. "Is that what it's like?" she asked. "After centuries, do experiences become... dulled?"

Devon thought about the question as they walked. "Not dulled, exactly," he said. "More categorized. The mind makes patterns, references, and comparisons. 'This snowfall is heavier than the one in 1857, lighter than the blizzard of 1923.' The experience gets placed in memory instead of being fully lived in the moment."

"That sounds lonely," Kate said. "To always be comparing instead of experiencing."

"It can be," Devon admitted. "It's one reason many of my kind seek novelty, sometimes destructively so. New experiences become precious when so much is familiar."

"What would you do?" Kate asked finally. "If you knew your time was limited, like humans do?"

Devon considered the question with evident care. "I would create more," he said after a long moment. "Music, primarily, but perhaps explore other forms as well. I would allow myself to form connections without the constant awareness of inevitable loss."

The admission revealed a vulnerability that touched Kate deeply. She understood now a fundamental paradox of Devon's existence, that immortality, rather than freeing him from the constraints of time, had in some ways imprisoned him in a state of emotional caution, always aware that human connections would end in loss.

"And what would you do differently," Devon asked, turning the question back to her, "if you had the time I do?"

Kate hadn't expected the reversal, so she took her time considering her answer. "I would learn more," she said finally. "I would travel more extensively, experience cultures more deeply. And I would…" she paused, searching for the right words, "I would worry less about wasting time, about making the 'right' choices."

Devon nodded, understanding in his eyes. "Two sides of the same coin," he observed. "I have too much time and thus lack urgency; you have too little and thus feel its pressure constantly."

"And here we are in the middle," Kate said softly, "each offering the other a different perspective."

The observation hung in the air between them, simple but profound. In that moment, Kate felt the unique balance they brought to each other's lives, her human perspective of limited time and urgent engagement counterpointing his immortal view of patience and historical context.

Devon reached out slowly, his hand finding hers. "Here we are."

Without thinking, she leaned up and kissed him gently, a spontaneous expression of the emotion his words had stirred in her. Devon's hand rose to cup her cheek in an intimate, adoring touch. When they separated, his eyes held hers with an intensity that spoke volumes.

"Stay with me tonight," he said softly. "Not in the chamber, not as part of any ritual or arrangement, but simply because we choose it."

The invitation was offered without pressure or expectation, a genuine choice rather than a seduction. Kate considered it briefly, then nodded, her decision made not from calculation or strategy but from the magnetic connection that had grown between them.

"I'd like that," she said simply.

They returned to the main house hand in hand, the snow falling around them in the quiet night. No further words were needed, they had moved beyond the need for constant verbal negotiation of boundaries and expectations, into a space of mutual understanding and trust that felt entirely natural.

When they reached his chambers, Devon turned to face her, his hands coming up to frame her waist with infinite gentleness. The silk of her dress felt cool beneath his palms, but he could feel the warmth of her skin beneath it, the rapid flutter of her pulse at her throat.

"Are you certain?" he asked quietly, his thumbs brushing across the fabric at her waist in slow, hypnotic circles. "We don't have to—"

Kate silenced him by rising on her toes to press her lips to his, a soft kiss that carried all her certainty, all her choice. Her hands fisted in the front of his shirt, pulling him closer, and when they separated, she kept her hands on his chest.

"I want this," she whispered, her breath warm against his lips. "I want you."

Devon's eyes closed briefly, committing her words to memory. When he opened them again, the intensity there made her breath catch, ancient eyes that had seen centuries pass, now focused entirely on her with devotion.

His hands moved to undo the buttons of her dress. The first button slipped free, then the second, his knuckles brushing against her collarbone with each careful movement. Kate watched his face as he undressed her, seeing the wonder there, the disciplined restraint, the profound gratitude that transformed his aristocratic features into something almost vulnerable.

"You are so beautiful," he murmured, his voice rough with emotion as the dress pooled at her feet like spilled midnight. His eyes traced every curve, every line of her body as if committing her to memory.

Kate's arms instinctively moved to cover herself, a flush spreading across her skin from her chest to her cheeks. Even after their first time together, being seen like this—completely exposed, vulnerable under his intense gaze— still felt overwhelming.

Her eyes dropped from his face, suddenly unable to meet that burning stare that seemed to see straight through her defences. Devon's hands gently caught her wrists, not pulling her arms away but simply holding them with infinite tenderness. His touch was warm, grounding, patient.

"Kate," he said softly, waiting until she reluctantly lifted her eyes to his. The intensity there should have made her more uncomfortable, but instead she saw only reverence, as if she were something sacred he'd been granted permission to worship. "You are safe with me," he said quietly, his forehead coming down to rest against hers in an intimate gesture. "Always. In every way."

Her breath hitched at the simple certainty in his voice, at the way his thumbs traced gentle circles on the sensitive skin of her wrists. Slowly, she let her arms fall to her sides, trusting him, trusting this moment between them.

"There," he whispered against her lips, his hands moving to frame her face with delicate care. "Let me see you. All of you."

Kate's hands moved to his shirt with trembling fingers, working at the buttons with timid hands. When the shirt fell away, she couldn't help but stare at the sight of him, pale and perfect, like a sculpture come to life, all lean muscle and masculine planes.

"Your turn," she whispered, her hands boldly moving to his belt.

Once they were both undressed, Devon led her to the bed. The silk sheets were cool against her heated skin as he lay her down gently. He settled beside her, propping himself up on one elbow, his free hand tracing the curve of her shoulder, her arm, her hip with feather-light touches that made her shiver.

"I want to learn you," he said softly, his fingers following the path his eyes traced across her skin. "Every sound you make, the way you respond to my touch. I want to memorize all of it."

Kate's breath caught as his hand moved lower, exploring with patient thoroughness. His touch was gentle but sure, finding sensitive spots she hadn't even known existed.

"I want that too," she managed, her own hand reaching up to trace the strong line of his jaw, the elegant curve of his neck. "I want to know what makes you… what you like…"

Devon caught her hand, bringing it to his lips to press a gentle kiss to her palm, then to each fingertip in turn. "Touch me," he said simply, his voice rough with barely contained desire. "However you want. I'm yours, Kate. Completely yours."

The simple honesty of the statement made her heart race. She began to explore him as he was exploring her, marveling at the contrast between his marble-pale skin and her warmer tones, at the way his muscles tensed under her touch, at the soft sounds he made when she found particularly sensitive spots. His skin was cool but warmed under her hands, and she could feel the careful control he maintained, the way he held himself back for her.

"Is this good?" she asked softly, her fingers trailing down his chest, tracing the defined lines of his abdomen, and Devon's eyes fluttered closed for a moment before opening to meet hers again.

"Everything you do is good," he said, his voice strained with restraint. His hand moved to cover hers, guiding her touch lower, his breath catching as her fingers drifted down his abdomen. "But this…" he breathed as her hand moved lower still, "this is divine."

Kate watched his face as she explored him, fascinated by the way his breath hitched when she touched him just so, the way his eyes darkened with desire, the way his careful control seemed to fray at the edges. "And this?" she whispered, her hand wrapping around him with gentle pressure.

"Heaven," he managed, his voice rough, his hips jerking involuntarily at her touch. "Kate, you're going to be the death of me."

She smiled at that, growing bolder in her exploration, learning what made him gasp, what made his eyes roll back, what made his hands fist in the sheets. "I thought you were already dead," she teased gently, her thumb brushing across the sensitive head of his cock.

Devon's laugh was breathless, strained, cut off by a sharp intake of breath as she continued her ministrations. "Not when you touch me like that. When you touch me, I feel more alive than I have in centuries."

Their exploration continued, unhurried and thorough, punctuated by soft conversations, gentle laughter, and increasingly heated kisses. Devon consumed her with his hands and mouth, his lips trailing fire across her skin as he mapped every inch of her body with adoration and attention.

His tongue circled her nipples with maddening precision, drawing them into peaks before grazing them with his teeth. Kate's hands tangled in his hair, her back arching as he alternated between gentle suction and the careful scrape of his teeth. When he pulled back slightly, she could see the hint of his fangs, elongated with desire, and fascination overcame her.

"Can I…?" she whispered, her finger reaching up to trace the sharp point of one fang with wondering touch.

Devon's eyes darkened further, a low growl rumbling in his chest at her gentle exploration. "Kate," he breathed, his voice rough with barely contained need. "You have no idea what you do to me."

"I want to know," she whispered. "I want to know everything about you."

Devon caught her finger between his lips, his tongue swirling around the digit before releasing it. "Then let me show you," he murmured, his lips beginning a slow journey down her body.

He kissed and licked his way down her torso, pausing to explore her ribs, her stomach, the sensitive skin of her hip bones. His hands spread her thighs with gentle pressure, and Kate's breath caught as she realized his intention.

"Devon," she whispered, suddenly shy despite everything they had already shared.

"Let me love you," he said simply, his eyes meeting hers with burning intensity. "Like you deserve."

His lips pressed delicate kisses to the inside of her thigh, working slowly upward with maddening patience. Kate's hands fisted in the sheets as his tongue traced a hot, wet path along her sensitive skin, each touch igniting a fire inside her.

"So soft," he murmured against her thigh, his breath hot against her skin. "So perfect."

Kate let out a cry as his tongue finally lapped at the apex of her thighs, causing her hips to buck uncontrollably at the wonderful feeling. Devon's hands kept her steady while he used his mouth to examine her, his tongue locating all of her tender spots and discovering what caused her to squirm, groan, and gasp beneath him.

"Devon, please," she gasped, her hands tangling in his hair as he brought her higher and higher with his skilled mouth.

But true to form, just as she felt herself approaching the edge, he pulled back, pressing gentle kisses to her inner thighs, letting her breathing slow before beginning his sweet torture again.

"Not yet," he murmured against her skin. "I want to savor you. I want to make this last."

Kate's response was a frustrated whimper that made Devon smile against her thigh.

"Your turn," she managed, tugging at his hair to bring him back up to her level.

Devon allowed himself to be pulled up, settling beside her as Kate began her own exploration of his body. Her lips traced the strong line of his jaw, her tongue darting out to taste his skin. She could feel the tension in his muscles, the careful control he maintained even as she drove him to distraction. Her mouth moved lower, kissing and licking her way down his chest, pausing to lavish attention on his nipples the way he had done to hers. Devon's sharp intake of breath encouraged her, and she grew bolder, her teeth grazing his skin just enough to make him groan.

"Kate," he warned, his voice strained as her mouth moved lower still.

"Let me," she whispered, her hand wrapping around his arousal as her lips pressed kisses to his hip bone. "Let me love you too."

When her mouth finally closed around him, Devon's control nearly splintered completely. His hands fisted in the sheets as she explored him with her tongue, learning what made him gasp, what made his hips jerk, what made those beautiful sounds fall from his lips.

"God, Kate," he groaned, his hand coming up to tangle gently in her hair.

She smiled around him, taking him deeper, reveling in the way his careful composure crumbled under her swirling tongue. But before she could bring him too close to the edge, Devon gently pulled her away, bringing her back up to kiss her deeply.

"I want to watch you," he murmured against her throat, his hand moving between her legs with expert precision. "I want to see your face when you fall apart for me. I want to see every expression, every moment of pleasure I can give you."

His fingers moved skillfully, finding the perfect spot that made her cry out. He built a rhythm that had her writhing beneath him. But just when she reached the edge, he would slow down and soften his touch, keeping her in that perfect space between need and fulfillment.

"Look at me," he said as Kate's eyes began to drift closed, overwhelmed by sensation. "I want to see everything you're feeling."

Kate found herself unable to look away. There was something sacred in this moment of complete vulnerability and trust. His eyes held hers as his fingers continued their gentle torment, building her higher and higher only to ease back again.

"I love the way you look at me," she whispered, her hand coming up to cover his where it rested against her cheek. "Like I'm something precious."

"You are," Devon said simply, his forehead coming down to rest against hers again. "You're everything precious to me."

The words broke something open inside her, and she pulled him down for a kiss that was desperate, hungry, full of all the love and need she couldn't put into words. When they broke apart, both breathing hard, she could see her own emotions reflected in his ancient eyes.

"Please," she whispered, her body trembling with desire. "I need you. Now."

Devon positioned himself above her, his eyes searching hers for any sign of hesitation. Finding none, only love and trust and desperate want, he entered her slowly, inch by careful inch, both of them gasping at the exquisite sensation.

"Kate," he breathed, his forehead dropping to rest against hers as he stilled, letting her adjust to him. "You feel so perfect. So warm, so tight... god, you're everything."

Kate's hands came up to frame his face, her thumbs brushing across his cheekbones as she savored the feeling of him inside her, filling her completely.

"Move," she whispered. "Please. I need you to move."

Devon's eyes never left hers as he began to move inside her, each thrust slow and deliberate. His hands framed her face, fingers threading through her hair as he watched every expression that crossed her features, every flutter of her eyelashes, every parting of her lips.

The angle was perfect, each movement sending waves of pleasure through her body. Devon maintained that maddening control, building her pleasure slowly, carefully, bringing her to the edge only to slow his movements, to press gentle kisses to her lips, to whisper words of love and devotion against her skin.

Kate's breath came in short gasps as he moved within her again, the rhythm building slowly toward something that felt less like mere physical release and more like transcendence. "Devon," she whispered, a desperate plea, a declaration of everything she felt for him.

"I know," he breathed against her lips, his own control beginning to fray at the edges. "I know, my love. Let go for me. Let me see you fall apart."

His hand moved between them, finding that perfect spot, and the combination of his touch and the perfect angle of his thrusts finally sent her over the edge. Kate shattered in his arms, her body arching beneath him as waves of pleasure crashed over her, his name falling from her lips amongst sobs of pleasure. Devon followed her over the edge moments later, his face buried in her neck as his own release claimed him, a low, satisfied growl reverberating in his throat as he poured himself into her.

They lay entwined in the afterglow of their intimate act, Devon's fingers tracing lazy patterns on Kate's bare shoulder, her head on his chest. The silence between them was comfortable, filled with the weight of what they had just shared.

Kate finally lifted her head to look at him, her hair falling like a curtain around them. "I've never experienced anything like that before," she admitted softly. "The way you… the way you made me wait, made me feel every moment…"

Devon's hand came up to cup her face again, his thumb brushing across her cheekbone with infinite tenderness. "Nor have I," he said, and the simple honesty of the statement made her heart swell.

She leaned into his touch, pressing a kiss to his palm. "What happens now?" she asked, the question that had marked so many transitions in their relationship.

"Now," Devon said, pulling her closer against him, "we rest. We hold each other. Tomorrow we face whatever comes together."

Kate settled back against his chest, feeling safer and more cherished than she had ever felt in her life. In Devon's arms, she had found not just passion, but sanctuary. Not just desire, but love. As she began to fall asleep, Kate could still feel Devon's fingers continue exploring her skin, as if he couldn't believe she was real, that she was his. In that touch, she felt the depth of his love, his gratitude, his promise to cherish what they had built together.

Tomorrow would bring new challenges. But tonight, they had this; perfect, sacred, theirs.

Chapter 14

The evening of the Midwinter Gathering inevitably arrived. Kate studied her reflection in the mirror. The emerald gown she had purchased in Budapest fit perfectly, its elegant lines complimenting her slender frame while the color brought out her eyes. She had styled her hair in a simple updo that emphasized the clean lines of her neck and shoulders, a deliberate choice, given the significance of necks in vampire society.

No collar would adorn her throat tonight. No mark would identify her as anyone's possession. She would attend as Devon's protégée, his artistic discovery, while knowing the truth of their relationship ran far deeper.

As Kate applied the finishing touches to her makeup, her thoughts drifted to the previous night and the intimacy she and Devon had shared. Their connection had deepened, creating a foundation of trust that would be put to the test tonight.

Trust. The word still triggered a reflexive caution in Kate. She found herself thinking about Jason, her fellow student at the Art Institute of Chicago and later her lover, who had seemed to understand her work so completely, who appreciated the raw emotion she channeled into her paintings.

Until the day she'd walked into a small gallery in Wicker Park and found her concepts, her techniques, her very artistic voice appropriated in his solo exhibition. Not direct copies, he had been too clever for that, but the essence of her work, the techniques she had developed over years of experimentation, presented as his own creative breakthrough.

When confronted, he had been unapologetic. "Art is conversation," he had said with that infuriating smile. "I was just continuing the dialogue we started."

The gallery owner had sided with Jason, along with several of their mutual friends. Kate had been labeled difficult and oversensitive. The betrayal had been professional, personal, and social. After that, Kate had guarded her work more carefully, shared her process less freely, kept potential collaborators at arm's length. The walls she had built around her creative and emotional life had served her well, protecting her from further exploitation while allowing her to develop her distinctive style without interference.

Until Devon. Until a vampire aristocrat had seen something in her work that resonated with his own centuries of experience, something that had compelled him to bring her into his world. First as captive, then as companion, now as partner in a relationship that defied conventional definition.

The irony wasn't lost on Kate. She had spent years protecting herself from human betrayal, only to find an unexpected connection with a being who wasn't human at all.

A soft knock at the door snapped her back to reality. "Ms Morgan?" Marcus called. "The car will be ready in fifteen minutes."

"Thank you, Marcus, I'll be down shortly." Kate replied.

She took a final look in the mirror, straightening her shoulders and lifting her chin. Whatever challenges awaited at the gathering, she would face them with the same resilience that had carried her through past betrayals.

When Kate descended the grand staircase, she found Devon waiting in the entrance hall. He cut an imposing figure in a perfectly tailored tuxedo that somehow managed to appear both contemporary and timeless, much like Devon himself. His eyes widened just a touch when he saw her, unmistakable admiration flickering in his gaze.

"You look incredible," he said simply as she reached the bottom of the stairs.

"As do you," Kate replied, taking in the full effect of Devon in formal wear. There was something almost otherworldly about his elegance, a reminder of his true nature that the familiarity of recent days had sometimes allowed her to forget.

Devon offered his arm, a gesture both courtly and reassuring. "Are you ready?" he asked, his voice pitched for her ears alone.

Kate placed her hand on his arm, drawing strength from the contact. "As ready as I'll ever be," she replied honestly.

Outside, a sleek black limousine waited, its engine purring quietly in the cold night air. Marcus held the door as Devon handed Kate into the vehicle, then followed her inside. As the car pulled away from the estate, Kate felt a momentary pang of regret for the intimate sanctuary they were leaving behind, the private world they had created together, now to be tested by the harsh realities of vampire society.

"Tell me more about what to expect," she said, breaking the silence that had fallen between them. "Beyond what we've already discussed."

Devon turned slightly in his seat to face her more directly. "The gathering will be held at the Buda Castle, in a section not open to the public," he explained."

"How many will be there?" Kate asked, trying to prepare herself mentally for the scale of the event.

"Perhaps two hundred vampires," Devon replied. "Most with human companions. The European houses will be most strongly represented, though some from further afield make the journey for these biannual gatherings."

Kate nodded, absorbing the advice. "What should I expect from them?"

"Curiosity, mostly," Devon replied. "A human presented as a protégée rather than a Pet is unusual enough to attract attention. Some will be merely interested, others potentially dismissive of a human artist regardless of talent. A few may be hostile to the very concept of a human being accorded such status."

"And how should I respond to them?" Kate asked.

Devon considered the question carefully. "With dignity," he said finally. "Neither apologetic nor confrontational. You are there by right of my patronage, but your talent and perspective are your own.

The advice made sense, aligning with Kate's own instincts about how to navigate the gathering. She would not pretend to be something she wasn't, would not affect subservience or artificial deference. She would be herself, an artist of genuine talent, a human of substance and dignity, a partner to Devon in ways that went beyond conventional categories.

As the limousine wound its way through the streets of Budapest toward the castle district, Kate found herself thinking again of Jason and the betrayal that had shaped her approach to relationships for years afterward. The pain had faded with time, but the lessons remained: protect oneself, don't trust easily, maintain boundaries and walls.

With Devon, those boundaries had dissolved, replaced by a different kind of protection. One based on mutual respect and understanding, rather than defensive distance.

"What are you thinking?" Devon asked softly, noting her pensive expression.

Kate hesitated, then decided to be honest. "About trust," she said. "About how difficult it can be to give, and how devastating it feel when it's betrayed."

Devon's expression grew thoughtful. "You speak from experience," he noted, not a question, but an invitation for her to share, if she wished.

Kate nodded slightly. "There was someone, years ago," she said. "A fellow artist who became... more. I trusted him with my work, my process, my creative voice. He took what I shared and presented it as his own innovation, his artistic breakthrough."

Devon's eyes darkened slightly, a flicker of anger on her behalf crossing his features. "What happened?" he asked.

"The art world sided with him," Kate replied, the old bitterness briefly resurfacing. "He was charismatic, well-connected. I was labeled difficult, possessive of ideas that should be 'part of the artistic dialogue.' I lost friends, opportunities, my place in a community I had valued."

"And so you learned to guard yourself more carefully," Devon concluded. "To protect your work and your heart with equal vigilance."

"Yes," Kate acknowledged. "Until you. Until this extraordinary situation that somehow led to... whatever we are to each other now."

Devon was silent for a moment, absorbing what she had shared. Then he reached for her hand, his touch gentle but firm. "Thank you," he said simply.

"For trusting me with this. For trusting me at all, given your experience."

The sincerity in his voice touched Kate deeply. "It hasn't been easy," she admitted. "Trusting again, especially under such unusual circumstances. But you've earned it, despite everything." Devon's expression softened. "I will endeavor to remain worthy of it," he said quietly.

The moment of connection hung between them, intimate and profound. Then the limousine began to slow, and Devon's expression shifted subtly, a mask of composed dignity settling over his features.

"We've arrived," he said, his voice taking on a formal quality that signaled the transition from private to public personas. "Remember, whatever happens tonight, whatever is said or implied, what exists between us is real. The rest is… necessary theater."

Kate nodded, understanding the distinction he was drawing. When the limousine came to a stop and the door was opened by an attendant, she took a deep breath and prepared herself for the role she was to play.

Devon exited first, then extended his hand to assist Kate from the vehicle. The Buda Castle loomed above them, its illuminated facade majestic against the night sky. They had been delivered to a private entrance, where other elegant vehicles were similarly discharging passengers, some human, some clearly not, all dressed in formal wear that ranged from contemporary to subtly archaic.

"Ready?" Devon asked quietly, offering his arm once more.

Kate placed her hand on his arm, drawing strength from the contact. "Ready," she whispered, as they approached the entrance.

The interior of the castle had been transformed for the gathering with subtle lighting and elegant decorations that respected the original architecture. Kate and Devon were greeted at the entrance by attendants who took their coats and directed them toward the main hall.

As they approached, Kate became aware of the subtle shift in Devon's demeanor. His expression changed to project confidence and authority. This was Devon the vampire aristocrat, Devon the respected member of an ancient society, a persona both familiar and strange to Kate after the intimacy they had shared.

"Remember," Devon murmured as they paused at the threshold of the main hall, "you are here by right of my patronage, but your worth is your own. Stand tall, speak when spoken to with confidence but not presumption, and above all, remain by my side unless I explicitly indicate otherwise."

Kate nodded slightly, appreciating the final reminder while noting its protective intent. Then they stepped forward together into the gathering of vampires and their human companions. The main hall was spectacular, a vast space with soaring ceilings and ornate chandeliers. Tall windows offered views of Budapest illuminated below. The crowd was perhaps a hundred and fifty figures, with more arriving behind Kate and Devon.

Kate was immediately able to distinguish between vampires and humans in the grand hall. The vampires were easy to spot by their confident demeanor and the subtle respect shown to them by the humans around them. And those humans, Kate noted with a mix of fascination and discomfort, all wore some type of collar. These elegant, often beautiful adornments clearly marked them as possessions rather than partners. In a shadowy alcove at the side of the hall, a vampire held his Pet against the wall, his head bent towards her neck. The Pet's head was thrown back in a silent, ecstatic gasp, her fingers gripping his velvet jacket as he fed. It wasn't violent or a struggle; it was an act of intense, almost sacred intimacy that felt more private than a kiss. Kate quickly looked away, feeling like a voyeur, a blush rising to her cheeks.

As Kate and Devon moved further into the hall, conversations paused briefly, heads turning to observe their arrival. Kate felt the weight of curious gazes, some merely interested, others more calculating. She kept her composure, her hand resting lightly on Devon's arm as they proceeded toward a group of vampires who had clearly noted their arrival.

"Devon," greeted a tall, silver-haired vampire with an aristocratic bearing that suggested centuries of privilege. "How good of you to join us this year. You've been missed at recent gatherings."

"Nikolai," Devon replied with a slight inclination of his head that suggested respect without subservience. "Circumstances have kept me occupied at the estate. May I present Katherine Morgan, an American artist of exceptional talent who is currently under my patronage."

Kate noted the careful phrasing, neither claiming her as a Pet nor explicitly acknowledging their true relationship. She offered a polite smile as Nikolai's gaze shifted to her, his assessment both thorough and unabashed.

"Ms Morgan," he acknowledged with old-world courtesy. "Your reputation precedes you. Aleksander mentioned that Devon had taken an interest in your work."

The mention of Aleksander sent a small chill through Kate. "You're acquainted with Mr Voss?" she asked, keeping her tone neutral.

"For several centuries," Nikolai confirmed with a thin smile. "Though 'acquainted' might be a generous term for our association. Aleksander moves in several circles and cultivates many… connections."

The statement spoke volumes about Nikolai's opinion of Aleksander, none of it particularly flattering.

"Ms Morgan's work explores themes of isolation and connection," Devon interjected smoothly, redirecting the conversation toward safer ground. "Her perspective on human emotional complexity has proven illuminating."

"How fascinating," Nikolai replied, though his tone suggested polite interest rather than genuine enthusiasm. "And you find vampire society instructive for your artistic development?"

The question carried subtle implications. Was Kate here merely as an observer, studying them like specimens for her art? Kate chose her words carefully. "I find all societies instructive," she replied diplomatically. "The power dynamics, how relationships form within those structures. These are universal themes that transcend species."

Nikolai's eyebrows rose slightly, suggesting her answer had been more sophisticated than he'd expected from a human. "Indeed," he murmured. "Universal themes. How… academic of you."

While Nikolai and Devon engaged in small talk, Kate's gaze drifted towards a dark corner to her left. She noticed a female vampire with her back pressed against the ancient stone, holding her Pet close. His hands were tangled in her hair as she fed from his neck, his collar pulled aside. Kate quickly redirected her attention to Nikolai, hoping her blush wasn't visible in the dim light.

Their conversation was interrupted by the approach of another vampire, this one accompanied by a human woman whose collar was a work of art in itself, delicate gold filigree that complemented rather than concealed the elegant lines of her neck.

"Nikolai, Devon," the newcomer greeted with evident warmth. "And this must be the famous protégée we've all been hearing about."

"Lucien," Devon acknowledged with genuine pleasure. "Kate, may I present Lucien Beaumont, an old friend from Paris. And this is Celeste."

Kate studied the human woman with interest. She carried herself with quiet confidence. Her collar, while clearly marking her status, seemed to be worn with pride rather than resignation. When she spoke, her voice was cultured, intelligent.

"Ms Morgan," Celeste said with a slight curtsy that managed to be respectful without being servile. "Lucien has told me about your work. I was an art history student before…" she gestured gracefully to her collar, "before my circumstances changed. I'd be honored to discuss your artistic process, if you're willing."

The request was unexpected, and Kate found herself genuinely intrigued by this articulate, educated woman who seemed to have found a place within vampire society that preserved her intellectual identity despite her status as Pet.

"I'd like that very much," Kate replied sincerely. "Perhaps later this evening?"

"I would be delighted," Celeste responded, her smile warm and genuine.

As the conversation continued, Kate noted that Lucien and Celeste's relationship seemed to be built on genuine affection and mutual respect. Celeste participated in the conversation as an equal, her opinions sought and valued by both vampires present.

Yet even as Kate observed this more positive example of the Pet system, she couldn't ignore the darker elements she'd witnessed. Throughout the hall Kate could see humans whose body language spoke of resignation, fear, or worse, a kind of hollow emptiness that suggested their spirits had been broken entirely.

"You seem thoughtful," Devon murmured as they moved away from Lucien and Celeste to greet other guests.

"I'm trying to understand," Kate replied quietly. "The relationships here are more complex than I expected. Some seem genuinely caring, others…" she trailed off, not wanting to voice her concerns in such a public setting.

"The Pet system, like any social structure, encompasses a wide range of individual experiences," Devon said. "Some vampires treat their companions with care and respect. Others…" his expression darkened slightly, "others view them as little more than livestock."

The blunt assessment confirmed Kate's observations. As they continued to circulate through the gathering, she found herself studying each vampire-human pair with new eyes, trying to understand the dynamics at play.

Near the center of the hall, she observed a vampire engaged in animated conversation with several peers. At his side stood a young man who couldn't have been more than twenty, his collar a simple band of black leather that seemed almost austere compared to the ornate adornments worn by other Pets. What struck Kate most forcefully was the young man's expression, or rather, the lack thereof. His eyes were vacant, his posture perfectly still, as if he were a beautifully crafted robot rather than a living person.

"That's disturbing," Kate murmured, unable to look away from the scene.

Devon followed her gaze, his expression growing grim. "Heinrich von Staufen," he said quietly. "One of the old German houses. His methods of training Pets are considered extreme even by traditional standards."

"Training?" Kate asked, though she suspected she didn't want to know the answer.

"Breaking might be a more accurate term," Devon replied, his voice tight with distaste. "Heinrich believes Pets should be seen and not heard, should exist solely for their master's pleasure and convenience."

Kate felt a chill run through her as she watched the young man's vacant stare. Whatever had been done to him had effectively erased his personality, leaving behind only a beautiful shell. The sight made her grateful for Devon's respect towards her autonomy and dignity.

"How is that allowed?" she asked.

"Vampire society values individual autonomy," Devon explained. "Each vampire is considered sovereign within their own domain, free to manage their affairs as they see fit. Interference in another's relationship with their Pet is considered a grave breach of protocol."

"Even when it involves what amounts to psychological torture?"

"Even then," Devon confirmed grimly.

Their conversation was interrupted by the approach of Aleksander Voss. He was impeccably dressed and wearing a characteristic smile that didn't quite meet his eyes. "Devon, Ms Morgan," he greeted with a slight bow. "I trust you're finding the gathering... educational?"

"Illuminating," Kate replied carefully, noting how Aleksander's gaze seemed to catalog every detail of her appearance and demeanor.

"I'm sure it is," Aleksander agreed. "So few humans have the opportunity to observe our society from the inside. Your perspective as an artist must make it particularly fascinating."

"I find all social interactions fascinating," she replied diplomatically.

"Indeed," Aleksander murmured. "And what do you make of our particular... structures? The Pet system, for instance. How does it strike your artistic sensibilities?"

The question was clearly designed to elicit a reaction. She chose her words carefully. "Like any social system, it seems to encompass a wide range of individual experiences," she said, echoing Devon's earlier assessment. "Some relationships appear to be built on genuine care and mutual benefit, while others..." she paused, glancing toward Heinrich and his vacant-eyed companion, "others seem less balanced."

Aleksander followed her gaze, his smile widening slightly. "Ah, you've noticed Heinrich's latest acquisition. Beautiful, isn't he? Though perhaps not quite as animated as some might prefer."

The casual cruelty in his tone made Kate's stomach turn, but she maintained her composed expression. "I prefer my companions to keep their personalities," she said quietly.

"How refreshingly modern of you," Aleksander replied with apparent amusement. "I wonder if you'll maintain that perspective as you spend more time in our world. Humans can be so… unpredictable when left to their own devices."

Before Kate could respond, Devon stepped slightly closer to her side, a subtle but clear signal of protection. "Kate's unpredictability is one of her most valuable qualities," he said smoothly. "Predictable humans make for predictable art, and predictable art is rarely worth preserving."

The exchange was polite on the surface, but Kate recognized the subtle power struggle underneath, Aleksander testing boundaries, Devon establishing them firmly without direct confrontation.

"Of course," Aleksander conceded with a slight tilt of his head. "Another time, perhaps. Ms Morgan, it has been a pleasure. I look forward to continuing our conversation… when circumstances permit."

With that, he moved away, seamlessly joining another group of vampires across the hall. Devon watched him go, his expression revealing nothing of his thoughts.

"He's persistent," Kate observed quietly.

"Aleksander has always excelled at identifying what others value and finding ways to acquire it for himself," Devon replied, his voice equally low. "Whether through charm, negotiation, or more… direct methods."

The warning was clear, reinforcing Kate's own instinctive wariness of Aleksander's interest. "I'll be careful," she assured Devon.

"We both will," he responded, offering his arm once more. "Come. There are others I should introduce you to before the formal proceedings begin."

As they moved through the gathering, Kate was introduced to more members of vampire society, some cordial, some coolly polite, a few openly curious about her status as protégée rather than Pet.

As the evening progressed, a subtle shift in the gathering's energy alerted Kate that something was changing. Conversations quieted, attention turning toward the far end of the hall where a small raised platform had been arranged. Devon guided Kate in that direction, his expression suggesting that an important part of the evening's proceedings was about to begin.

"The formal acknowledgments," he explained quietly as they found a place with a clear view of the platform. "A tradition at each gathering; recognition of significant events, achievements, and changes in status within our society since the previous meeting."

Kate nodded her understanding, noting how the vampires arranged themselves with clear attention to hierarchy, the most prominent figures positioned closest to the platform, others arrayed behind them in what appeared to be order of status or influence.

A tall, austere vampire with silver-streaked dark hair and an air of absolute authority ascended the platform, his presence immediately commanding complete silence from the gathering. Even the human Pets seemed to sense the shift in atmosphere, their posture becoming more formal, their expressions more subdued.

"That is Viktor Dracul," Devon murmured, his voice so low that only Kate could hear. "One of the oldest among us, and the nominal head of the European houses. His lineage traces back to the original Dracul family of Wallachia."

Kate absorbed this information with interest, studying the ancient vampire who now addressed the gathering. Viktor spoke first in what Kate recognized as Latin, then switched to English, a concession, she suspected, to the international nature of the gathering.

The acknowledgments began with formal recognition of new vampires created since the previous gathering, a process, Kate gathered, that was carefully regulated and required approval from the Vampire Council. Then came acknowledgment of significant achievements, artistic works, scientific contributions, business successes that had enhanced the collective wealth and influence of vampire society.

Viktor recognized contributions spanning fields from medical research to environmental conservation, from technological innovation to preservation of cultural heritage. The breadth of vampire involvement in human affairs was greater than Kate had imagined, their influence extending into virtually every sphere of human activity, largely unrecognized by the societies they moved through.

Then came what appeared to be the most socially significant portion of the acknowledgments; recognition of new or changed relationships between vampires and humans. Viktor acknowledged several new humans who had been formally accepted as Pets by vampires of significant standing. Each vampire and their new human companion stepped forward briefly, the human's collar clearly displaying their status.

As the relationship acknowledgments continued, Kate became aware of a subtle shift in the atmosphere around her. Glances were being directed their way, whispers exchanged behind discreetly raised hands. Devon's expression remained impassive, but Kate sensed a tension in his posture that hadn't been present moments before.

Then Viktor's voice cut through her observations, the formal tones taking on a note of what might have been surprise or perhaps disapproval. "I understand there is one additional relationship to acknowledge," he said, his gaze sweeping the gathering before settling on Devon. "Devon Karlov has requested recognition of a human protégée, an unusual designation in recent centuries."

A murmur rippled through the gathering, Devon straightened slightly beside her, his chin lifting in subtle defiance of the whispers and stares.

"Devon Karlov," Viktor continued, "please present your protégée for acknowledgment."

Devon placed his hand gently at the small of Kate's back, guiding her forward with him as they approached the platform. Kate was acutely aware of every eye in the hall upon them, of the absence of a collar at her throat, of the subtle, but unmistakable difference in how they moved together, compared to the vampire-Pet pairs who had been acknowledged before them.

As they reached the platform, Devon spoke in clear, carrying tones that betrayed no hint of uncertainty or apology. "I present Katherine Morgan, American artist, whose work demonstrates exceptional insight into the human condition and whose talent merits recognition and development."

Viktor studied Kate with ancient eyes that seemed to see far more than her physical appearance. "Ms Morgan," he acknowledged with a slight inclination of his head. "It has been some time since a human has been presented as a protégée rather than a Pet at our gathering. The distinction carries… different expectations and responsibilities."

"I understand," Kate replied, her voice steady despite the intensity of the moment.

"Do you?" Viktor questioned, his tone suggesting genuine curiosity rather than challenge. "The role of protégée in our society has traditionally been one of apprentice to master. It implies a relationship of mentorship rather than ownership."

"Yes," Kate confirmed, maintaining eye contact. "That is my understanding of the arrangement."

Viktor's gaze shifted to Devon. "And you, Devon Karlov, accept the responsibilities of patron rather than master? You claim no ownership rights over this human, no exclusive access to her resources?"

The careful phrasing made the subtext clear: Viktor was asking whether Devon was renouncing the traditional vampire right to feed from a human companion, to exercise control and restraint.

"I accept the responsibilities of patron," Devon confirmed, his voice unwavering. "Ms Morgan's talent deserves nurturing on its own terms, not as an adjunct to my interests or needs."

Viktor was silent for a moment, his expression unreadable as he looked between Devon and Kate. Then he nodded slightly, a gesture that seemed to carry significant weight given the hushed attention of the gathering.

"The protégée relationship between Devon Karlov and Katherine Morgan is acknowledged," he declared formally. "Ms Morgan will be accorded the respect due to one under the patronage of House Karlov, with the freedoms and responsibilities that status entails."

Another murmur swept through the gathering, this one with notes of surprise, curiosity, and in some quarters, what sounded like disapproval. Kate maintained her composed expression, neither triumphant nor apologetic, as she and Devon stepped back from the platform.

As they moved away, Kate became aware of Aleksander watching them from across the hall, his expression a complex mixture of calculation and what might have been grudging admiration. Their eyes met briefly, and he raised his glass in a subtle toast that felt more like a challenge than a congratulation.

"That was… intense," Kate murmured as they rejoined the general gathering, which was now dispersing into smaller groups as the formal acknowledgments concluded.

"Viktor rarely speaks so directly," Devon replied quietly. "His interest suggests our arrangement has implications beyond what I anticipated."

Before Kate could ask what those might be, they were approached by a striking vampire woman whose age was impossible to determine. She might have been thirty or three hundred, her features timeless in their elegant symmetry. At her side was a human man in his early thirties, wearing a collar of intricate silver links that complemented rather than concealed the strong lines of his neck and shoulders.

"Devon," the vampire woman greeted with warmth. "How delightful to see you emerging from your self-imposed isolation. And with such an interesting companion."

"Sophia," Devon acknowledged, genuine pleasure in his tone. "It has been too long. May I present Katherine Morgan, artist and protégée. Kate, this is Sophia Renard, one of the few among us I would genuinely call a friend rather than merely ally."

Kate noted the distinction as she exchanged greetings with Sophia. She was more genuinely welcoming than most of the vampires she had met that evening.

"And this is Thomas," Sophia continued, indicating the human man beside her. "My companion of fifteen years now."

Kate noted that Sophia used "companion" rather than "Pet," a subtle but significant distinction that suggested a relationship more nuanced than simple ownership. Thomas inclined his head politely, his expression neither subservient nor resentful, but rather comfortable with his place beside Sophia.

"Fifteen years," Devon remarked. "That's significant longevity for a human companion in our circles."

"We suit each other," Sophia replied simply, her hand resting briefly on Thomas's arm in a gesture that suggested genuine affection. "Though I confess, I've never considered the protégée designation. It's an intriguing alternative to traditional arrangements."

The conversation that followed was the most comfortable Kate had experienced since arriving at the gathering. Sophia asked thoughtful questions about Kate's work, showing genuine interest in her artistic process and perspective. Thomas contributed occasionally to the conversation, his comments suggesting both intelligence and a clear understanding of vampire society's complexities.

"I was a graduate student when I met Sophia," Thomas explained when Kate asked about his background. "Studying European history, actually. She offered me access to primary sources I could never have seen otherwise, letters, documents, firsthand accounts of events I'd only read about in textbooks."

"And in exchange?" Kate asked, genuinely curious about the dynamics of their relationship.

Thomas touched his collar unconsciously, a gesture that seemed more habitual than self-conscious. "Companionship. Blood, when she needs it. And..." he glanced at Sophia with obvious affection, "a life far more interesting than anything I could have imagined in academia."

"Thomas has become quite the scholar of vampire history," Sophia added with evident pride. "We're working on a book together, a comprehensive history of vampire-human relations over the centuries."

Kate found herself genuinely impressed by their partnership. It was perhaps the most positive example of the Pet system she had encountered at the gathering.

"You should visit us in Paris," Sophia suggested as the conversation drew to a natural close. "The artistic community might offer interesting opportunities for your work, Ms Morgan."

"I'd like that," Kate replied sincerely, finding in Sophia a potential ally she hadn't expected to encounter at the gathering.

As Sophia and Thomas moved away to greet other acquaintances, Devon leaned slightly closer to Kate. "Sophia represents a progressive faction within our society," he explained quietly. "Her interest in our arrangement is significant, potential support if challenges arise."

"Challenges?" Kate questioned. "You expect opposition to my status?"

"Not immediate or direct," Devon clarified. "But traditionalists like Viktor will be watching closely, evaluating whether our arrangement respects the fundamental separation they believe should exist between our kinds."

The reminder of the underlying tensions in vampire society sobered Kate. As she and Devon continued to circulate through the gathering, she was aware of the divided reactions to their acknowledged status.

And always, at the periphery of her awareness, was Aleksander, watching, evaluating, occasionally engaging in conversation with vampires who had just spoken with Devon and Kate, as if gathering impressions and information for some purpose of his own.

Kate began to feel fatigue in a way that had nothing to do with physical exhaustion and everything to do with the mental strain of navigating unfamiliar social waters. Devon, attuned to her state as always, guided them toward a quieter area of the hall. "You're doing remarkably well," he said quietly.

"It's fascinating," Kate admitted. "Disturbing in some ways, but fascinating. The complexity of the relationships, the political currents beneath the surface..."

"And yet you navigate it with natural grace," Devon observed. "Your artist's eye serves you well in reading the unspoken dynamics."

Kate was about to respond when a commotion near the center of the hall drew their attention. A young vampire, perhaps recently turned based on his apparent nervousness, had approached Heinrich von Staufen and was speaking in urgent, low tones. Heinrich's expression grew increasingly dark as he listened, and when the young vampire finished speaking, Heinrich's response was swift and violent.

The backhand blow sent the younger vampire staggering, drawing gasps from nearby observers. But what made Kate's blood run cold was Heinrich's reaction to his Pet, the vacant-eyed young man who had remained motionless throughout the exchange. Heinrich grabbed the young man roughly, his grip clearly painful, hissing something in German.

The Pet flinched, his expression remaining eerily blank even as Heinrich's grip tightened enough to leave bruises. It was a display of casual cruelty that made Kate feel sick, a reminder of the darker possibilities inherent in the Pet system.

"We should go," Devon said quietly, noting Kate's distress. "You've seen enough for one evening."

Kate nodded, grateful for his understanding. Waiting for their limousine, Kate reflected on the evening's revelations. She had expected to find a clear hierarchy of predator and prey. Instead, she had discovered a complex social structure. Some vampires were indeed predators in the worst sense, but others seemed to genuinely care for their human companions.

On the way back to the estate, Devon was quieter than usual. His expression was thoughtful as he gazed out at the nighttime cityscape of Budapest. Kate respected his silence, understanding that the evening had been significant for him as well.

The tension that had characterized much of the evening had eased from his shoulders, replaced by a quiet thoughtfulness that made him seem more accessible, more human despite his immortal nature. "What are you thinking?" she asked softly, breaking the comfortable silence between them.

Devon turned to her. "That I've existed for centuries," he replied, his voice soft, "attended countless gatherings, navigated innumerable social and political complexities. And yet tonight felt entirely new, because I experienced it with you."

Without conscious thought, Kate moved across the space separating them, closing the distance both physical and metaphorical that had been necessary during their public performance.

"We handled that well," she said softly, her hand seeking his in the low light of the limousine. "The two of us."

"Yes," Devon murmured, lacing his fingers with hers. "The two of us."

The words lingered between them, heavy with meaning that reached far deeper than they appeared. Then Devon lifted his other hand, brushing his fingertips along Kate's cheek with a tenderness that stole the air from her lungs.

"May I?" he asked, his gaze dropping briefly to her lips.

In answer, Kate leaned forward, closing the remaining distance between them. Their kiss began softly, a gentle affirmation of connection after the strain of the evening. But it quickly deepened, the tension and restraint of the gathering transforming into a different kind of intensity, one born of genuine desire rather than social performance.

Kate's hands found their way to Devon's shoulders, then to the nape of his neck, drawing him closer as the kiss continued. His own hands settled at her waist, steady and sure, neither possessive nor hesitant but perfectly balanced in their touch.

When they finally separated, Kate found herself smiling. "I've been wanting to do that all evening," she admitted, her voice low and intimate in the confined space.

"As have I," Devon confessed, his own smile matching hers in its authenticity. "Watching you navigate vampire society with such grace, such natural dignity, it was incredibly difficult for me to maintain the appropriate distance."

"Appropriate distance," Kate echoed with a soft laugh. "I think we've moved well beyond that, wouldn't you say?"

Devon responded by drawing her closer once again, his kiss this time more confident and passionate, a clear statement of exactly how far beyond "appropriate distance" they had traveled together. They remained entwined for the remainder of the journey, exchanging kisses and gentle touches that spoke more eloquently than words of the connection that had grown between them.

By the time the estate came into view, its lights welcoming in the darkness, Kate felt a sense of homecoming that would have been unimaginable during her early days of captivity.

Whatever challenges Aleksander might present, whatever complications vampire society might impose on their relationship, she and Devon had established something genuine between them, a foundation strong enough to withstand external pressures and internal doubts.

The gathering had been a test, and they had passed it together. Not without cost or complication, but with a unity of purpose and mutual support that boded well for whatever lay ahead. A unity now affirmed through the physical expression of their deepening bond.

Chapter 15

The days following the Midwinter Gathering unfolded with a quiet intimacy. Inside the sanctuary of the estate, Kate and Devon explored the growing connection that had been tested and affirmed by their public debut in vampire society.

They enjoyed the peaceful interlude at the estate for just over a week before reality intruded in the form of an elegant cream-colored envelope delivered by courier. The envelope's seal bore the Voss family crest, a stylized wolf's head surrounded by ancient runes.

Kate was in her studio, working on a new painting that explored the interplay of light and shadow when Devon found her. His expression was carefully neutral in a way that immediately told her that something was wrong.

"What is it?" she asked directly. She set down her brush and wiped her paint-stained hands on a nearby cloth.

Devon held up the envelope that he had already opened. "An invitation," he said in a calm tone. "From Aleksander. He's hosting a gathering at his Budapest residence tomorrow evening. Our presence is specifically requested."

Kate felt a chill at the wording. In the week since the Midwinter Gathering, she had hoped that Aleksander's interest would fade, and that the political maneuvering would settle into a more manageable pattern. Clearly, she had been naive.

"Requested or required?" she asked. She suspected she already knew the answer.

"There's often little difference in vampire society," Devon replied, handing her the invitation. "Especially when the request comes from someone of Aleksander's standing."

The card was heavy, expensive stock, the text engraved rather than printed. Kate read it quickly, noting the formal language and the deliberate mention of both her and Devon by name, along with a phrase that made her stomach tighten: "A celebration of artistic patronage and the evolution of vampire-human relationships."

"This isn't a coincidence," she said, looking up to meet Devon's gaze. "He's making this about us specifically."

"Deliberately so," Devon agreed, his expression growing more serious. "Aleksander is making a move, but we're not sure what it is yet. The theme suggests he plans to challenge our arrangement in public, to force some kind of confrontation or demonstration."

Kate set the invitation down on her work table and studied Devon's face. She could see the tension beneath his composed exterior, the way his jaw tightened slightly when he was weighing difficult options.

"Do we have to attend?" she asked, though she was starting to grasp the answer.

Devon was silent for a moment, considering the question with his usual care. "Technically, no," he said finally. "But refusing would be interpreted as weakness or fear. It would damage our position in vampire society and potentially embolden Aleksander to more direct action. He might interpret our absence as an admission that our arrangement is indeed as fragile as he suspects."

"So we go," Kate concluded, "and face whatever he has planned. Aleksander doesn't understand what he's up against."

"And what is that?" Devon asked in a whisper.

Kate lifted her head to meet his gaze. "Us," she said simply. "Together. A partnership built on choice, respect, and real feeling. He can't create that through manipulation or pressure, no matter how smart his method."

"Together," he agreed, the word holding all the weight of their shared commitment.

He walked deeper into the studio and looked at the canvas Kate had been working on. "This is remarkable," he said, trying to set the matter aside, at least for now.

Kate watched him as he examined her work, noting the way the moonlight from the studio windows played across his features, highlighting the strong line of his jaw, the elegant curve of his neck. A delicious idea began to form in her mind, artistic and intimate in equal measure, a tempting distraction from the unwelcome invitation.

"Take off your shirt," she said quietly, her voice carrying a note of gentle command that made Devon's eyes snap to hers.

"Kate?" he questioned, though she could see the immediate spark of interest in his gaze.

"I want to paint you," she explained, reaching for a clean brush and palette. "Not a portrait, something more abstract. I want to capture the way light moves across your skin."

Devon's eyes darkened with understanding and desire. "Here? Now?"

"Here. Now." Kate's voice was steady, but her pulse quickened as she watched him consider her request. "Your pants too."

Without breaking eye contact, Devon began unbuttoning his shirt with deliberate slowness. Kate felt her breath catch as each button revealed more of his pale, perfectly sculpted chest. When he shrugged the shirt off his shoulders, she had to remind herself to breathe.

His hands moved to his belt, and Kate watched, transfixed, as he removed his pants with the same unhurried grace. He stood nude before her, magnificent and unashamed, his body a study in unholy perfection that made her artist's eye sing with appreciation.

"Beautiful," she whispered, loading her brush with deep blue paint. "Now hold still."

She approached him slowly, the brush poised in her hand. When the first stroke of paint touched his chest, just above his heart, Devon's sharp intake of breath was audible in the quiet studio.

"Kate," he breathed, his voice already rough with arousal.

"Shh," she murmured, concentrating on her work. She drew the brush across his collarbone in a long, sweeping stroke, watching the way his muscles tensed beneath her touch. The paint was cool against his skin, but she could feel the heat radiating from his body.

Each stroke of the brush became a caress, deliberate and sensual. She painted abstract patterns across his chest, swirls and lines that followed the contours of his muscles. When she drew the brush down the center of his torso, Devon's hands clenched at his sides, his breathing becoming more labored.

"You're enjoying this," Kate observed, her voice husky as she noticed the obvious evidence of his arousal.

The best Devon could do without losing all control was roll his head back and nod yes in exquisite torture, his eyes fastened tight.

Kate smiled, loading her brush with gold paint this time. She traced it along his ribs, watching him shiver at the sensation. "I love watching you react," she said softly. "Seeing what affects you, what makes you lose that perfect control."

She painted spirals around his nipples, the brush barely touching his skin, but enough to make him gasp. His hands moved as if to reach for her, but she stepped back slightly.

"Not yet," she said, her eyes meeting his. "I'm not finished."

The next stroke was bolder, a sweep of crimson paint that curved from his shoulder down to his hip. Devon's breathing became ragged, his usual composure completely shattered by the intimate artistry of her touch.

"Kate, please," he said, his voice breaking slightly.

She set down her brush and stepped back to admire her work. His torso was a canvas of color now, abstract patterns that somehow captured both his strength and his vulnerability. But more than that, she could see the effect her artistic touch had on him, the way his chest rose and fell rapidly, the tension in his muscles, the desire burning in his eyes.

"Perfect," she whispered, then reached for the hem of her shirt.

Devon watched, transfixed, as she pulled it over her head and let it fall to the floor. Their breathing was synchronized now, both of them caught in the web of desire they had woven together.

In one fluid movement, Devon closed the distance between them, his paint-covered hands framing her face as he kissed her with desperate hunger. He lifted her with vampiric grace, her legs wrapping instinctively around his waist as he pressed her back against the studio wall.

Kate gasped as he hitched her skirt up, his hands rough and urgent now. The cool wall against her back contrasted sharply with the heat of his body pressed against her front. When he pulled her panties aside, she was already ready for him, her body responding to the intimate artistry they had shared.

He entered her in one powerful thrust, both of them crying out at the intensity of the connection.

"Yes," Kate breathed, her nails digging into his shoulders as he moved within her with relentless intensity. The paint on his chest smeared against her skin, marking her as surely as she had marked him.

Devon's movements were powerful, almost violent in their passion, each thrust driving her higher against the wall. The sound of their bodies slapping together filled the studio, raw and primal and utterly consuming. This wasn't the gentle lovemaking they had shared before. This was primal, desperate, a claiming that bordered on the edge of pain and pleasure.

"Mine," he growled against her throat, his fangs grazing her skin without breaking it. "My Kate."

"Yours," she gasped, her body arching against his as the pleasure built to an almost unbearable peak. "Always yours."

As Devon's fangs grazed her neck again, Kate felt a surge of desperate need that went beyond the physical pleasure already consuming her. "Bite me." she gasped, her voice breathless with desire.

Devon's movements stilled for a moment, his eyes meeting hers with concern. "Are you certain?" he asked, his voice rough with barely contained hunger.

The raw need in her voice, the absolute trust in her eyes, broke down his resistance. "Yes," Kate breathed, tilting her head to expose more of her neck. "I want this. I want you. All of you."

With a low growl of surrender, Devon's fangs pierced the delicate skin of her neck. Kate cried out, but not in pain; the sensation was electric, a sharp pleasure that intensified every other sensation coursing through her body. The dual stimulation of his bite and thrusts sent her spiraling toward a climax more intense than anything she had ever experienced.

"Oh God, Devon," she gasped, her body convulsing around him as the combined pleasures overwhelmed her senses. The feeling of him feeding from her while moving within her was intoxicating, primal, a connection that went beyond the physical into something almost spiritual.

Devon groaned against her neck, the taste of her blood on his tongue driving him to the very edge of control. The intimacy of feeding from her while they were joined so completely was overwhelming, a claiming that marked her as his in the most fundamental way possible.

The climax hit them both like a physical blow, Kate crying out as her body convulsed around him, Devon's roar of completion muffled against her neck as he buried himself deep inside her. The dual sensations of his release and the gentle pull of his feeding sent aftershocks through Kate's body, leaving her trembling and gasping.

As their breathing began to slow, Devon carefully withdrew his fangs, immediately cleaning the small wounds with his tongue. He was meticulous in his care as he tended to her neck, gentle and thorough as he licked away every drop of blood. The intimacy of the act was almost as intense as what they had just shared, a tender aftercare that spoke of his deep concern for her wellbeing.

They clung to each other, shuddering with the aftershocks, paint, sweat, and the lingering taste of copper mingling between them. For long moments, they remained pressed against the wall, both breathing heavily, neither willing to break the intimate connection. Finally, Devon lowered her gently to her feet, though he kept his arms around her, supporting her trembling legs.

"That was…" Kate began, then trailed off, unable to find words for what they had just shared.

"Necessary," Devon finished, his voice still rough as he tilted her chin up to meet his eyes. "Perfect. You."

Kate looked down at herself, seeing the abstract patterns of paint now decorating her skin where their bodies had pressed together. "We're quite the masterpiece," she said with a breathless laugh.

Devon's eyes followed her gaze, taking in the way the paint had transferred from his body to hers, creating new patterns, new art from their passion. "The most beautiful collaboration I've ever been part of," he said seriously.

Kate reached up to touch his face, leaving a small smudge of blue paint on his cheek. "I love you," she said simply. He took her hand and pressed it firmly against his face. "I love you too," he said. "More than I thought possible. More than I've ever loved anything in my whole life."

* * *

Aleksander's Budapest residence was a striking contrast to Devon's estate. Where the estate was historic, organic, and integrated with its natural surroundings, Aleksander's home was aggressively modern, a glass and steel structure perched on the Buda hillside like a predator surveying its territory.

The architecture spoke of wealth, power, and a deliberate rejection of tradition, all qualities Kate had come to associate with Aleksander himself.

As their car wound up the hillside approach, Kate felt Devon's hand tighten slightly around hers, a rare physical tell that betrayed his tension despite his outwardly calm appearance.

"Remember," he said quietly as they neared the entrance, "whatever happens tonight, whatever is said or implied, what exists between us is real. Everything else is theater, necessary, perhaps, but it does not diminish the truth of our connection."

Kate nodded, recognizing the echo of his words before the Midwinter Gathering. But tonight felt different, more targeted and personal, with higher stakes despite the event's smaller scale.

The entrance to Aleksander's residence was a study in calculated prestige with soaring glass walls, dramatic lighting that turned the structure into a beacon against the night sky, artwork visible through the transparent walls that managed to be both valuable and provocative. Kate recognized pieces by several contemporary artists whose work commanded seven-figure sums, displayed with museum-quality precision but somehow lacking the warmth and integration she had found in Devon's collection.

Aleksander himself greeted them at the threshold, impeccably dressed in a suit that managed to be both classic and subtly avant-garde. His smile was warm, his manner welcoming, though Kate noted the calculating assessment in his pale green eyes as they moved from her to Devon and back again.

"Devon, Ms Morgan," he greeted them with apparent pleasure. "How good of you to come. You're among the last to arrive; we've been eagerly awaiting your presence to complete our gathering."

The phrasing suggested significance beyond mere social courtesy, a hint that their arrival was central to whatever Aleksander had planned for the evening. Devon inclined his head slightly, his expression revealing nothing of his thoughts.

"Aleksander," he acknowledged. "An intriguing invitation. The theme of artistic patronage is, after all, a subject of mutual interest."

"Indeed," Aleksander agreed, his smile widening slightly. "Though our approaches differ somewhat, don't they? Your... protégée arrangement has been the subject of considerable discussion since the Midwinter Gathering. I thought it might be valuable to explore those differences more thoroughly."

Before Devon could respond, Aleksander turned his attention fully to Kate, his gaze appreciative but assessing.

"Ms Morgan, you look magnificent. That shade of blue brings out the fire in your eyes, quite striking."

"Thank you," Kate replied simply, neither encouraging nor rebuffing his attention. "Your home is impressive. The architecture is quite... bold."

"A recent acquisition," Aleksander explained, gesturing to the space around them. "I find that surroundings should evolve as one does. Static environments lead to static thinking, don't you agree? Tradition has its place, but innovation drives progress."

The comment seemed directed at both of them, though Kate sensed it contained a subtle critique of Devon's more traditional estate. Before either could respond, Aleksander continued, gesturing toward the main reception area beyond.

"Please, join the others. There are several guests I believe you'll find interesting, Ms Morgan, artists and patrons with perspectives that might broaden your understanding of the possibilities available to someone of your talent."

As they moved past him into the main reception area, Kate felt Aleksander's hand brush lightly against her bare shoulder, a touch that could have been accidental but that she suspected was deliberately provocative, a small test of boundaries. She gave no reaction, maintaining her composed expression as she and Devon entered the gathering.

The reception room was a vast open space with floor-to-ceiling windows offering nighttime views of Budapest illuminated below. Perhaps thirty guests were present, a carefully curated mixture of vampires and humans that Kate immediately recognized as different from the Midwinter Gathering. Here, the human companions displayed a wider range of relationships with their vampire patrons. Some wore traditional collars, others more subtle indicators of their status.

"Aleksander cultivates a more progressive image in certain circles," Devon murmured, noting her observation. "Though reality is often more complex than the appearance suggests."

Before Kate could respond, they were approached by a striking vampire woman whose features suggested Mediterranean origin, her apparent age impossible to determine as was typical of Devon's kind.

"Devon Karlov," she greeted him with evident pleasure. "It has been far too long. Budapest does not see you often enough these days."

"Eliana," Devon acknowledged, genuine warmth in his tone. "A pleasant surprise. I didn't expect to find you at Aleksander's gathering."

"Nor I you," she replied with a smile that suggested shared history. "But here we both are, drawn by curiosity perhaps? Or obligation?" Her gaze shifted to Kate, interest evident in her expression. "And this must be the artist whose work has captivated you so thoroughly. Aleksander has spoken of her with great… admiration."

"Katherine Morgan," Devon introduced her. "Kate, this is Eliana Devereux, an old friend and occasional ally in the complicated world of vampire politics."

"Ms Morgan," Eliana acknowledged with a slight inclination of her head. "Your reputation precedes you both, your artistic talent and your unique position in our society. The protégée designation has sparked considerable interest among the more progressive members of our community."

Kate noted the careful phrasing, neither explicitly approving nor condemning their arrangement but acknowledging its unconventional nature. "It's a pleasure to meet you," she replied. "Are you an art collector yourself?"

"Among other interests," Eliana confirmed. "Though my tastes run more to the classical than the contemporary."

The conversation that followed revealed Eliana to be both knowledgeable and thoughtful in her aesthetic perspectives, genuinely interested in Kate's artistic process and philosophical approach to her work. As they spoke, Kate became aware of Aleksander moving through the gathering with purposeful grace, engaging briefly with various guests while maintaining a subtle awareness of her and Devon's location and interactions.

There was orchestration in his movements, a sense of careful timing that suggested the evening was proceeding according to some plan only he fully understood. Devon seemed to sense it as well, his manner relaxed on the surface but with an underlying vigilance that Kate had come to recognize.

After perhaps forty minutes of circulating through the gathering, speaking with various guests who seemed genuinely interested in Kate's work and her perspective on the intersection of art and patronage, Aleksander called for attention by tapping a crystal glass with a silver knife. The conversations quieted immediately, all eyes turning to their host as he moved to a slightly elevated position near the center of the room.

"Friends, colleagues, esteemed guests," he began, his voice carrying effortlessly through the space with the practiced projection of someone accustomed to commanding attention. "Thank you for joining me this evening for what I hope will be a memorable exploration of the relationship between art, patronage, and power in our evolving society."

Kate felt Devon's subtle shift beside her, a barely perceptible tightening of his posture that suggested heightened alertness. This was the moment they had been preparing for, the confrontation Aleksander had been orchestrating since their arrival.

"Art has always been central to vampire society," Aleksander continued, his gaze sweeping the gathering with practiced ease. "Not merely as decoration or investment, but as a means of capturing and preserving the human experience that we ourselves have transcended. We collect it, commission it, occasionally create it ourselves, but always we are drawn to its ability to express emotions and perspectives that our own extended existence sometimes... dulls."

There were murmurs of agreement from several of the vampires present, nods of understanding at what appeared to be a commonly acknowledged aspect of immortal existence.

"This fascination with human creativity has led to various forms of patronage throughout our history," Aleksander went on, his tone becoming more pointed. "From the Renaissance masters who painted our portraits in exchange for protection and gold, to the modern arrangements that bring human artists directly into our households, our society has always sought ways to nurture and preserve human artistic expression."

His gaze settled on Kate and Devon, the focus of his remarks becoming unmistakably clear. "Recently, we have seen the emergence of new forms of patronage, arrangements that challenge traditional structures while claiming to better serve both vampire and human interests. The protégée designation, for instance, represents a fascinating evolution in how we conceptualize these relationships."

Kate felt the weight of every gaze in the room turning toward her and Devon. This was it, the public examination of their relationship that they had anticipated and prepared for.

"I find myself curious," Aleksander continued, his tone deceptively casual. "about the practical implications of such arrangements. The protégée designation suggests a relationship based on choice rather than ownership, on mutual benefit rather than service. But how does this translate to the more intimate aspects of vampire-human relationships? The exchange of blood, for instance, has traditionally been both a right and a necessity for vampire patrons."

The question lingered in the air like a challenge, its meaning clear to everyone present. Aleksander was asking Kate to publicly show the nature of her relationship with Devon, to confirm or deny the blood-sharing that was usually central to vampire-human partnerships.

Kate paused to think about her response, aware of the layers of manipulation in Aleksander's challenge. To refuse would suggest distance between her and Devon, which could undermine their position in vampire society. To agree too quickly might seem like subservience instead of choice, going against the independence implied by her protégée status.

"An interesting question," she said finally, her voice steady and clear in the now-silent room. "Though I wonder why my private choices should require public demonstration. In human society, we generally consider intimate acts between consenting adults to be their own business."

A ripple of reactions moved through the gathering, surprise at her directness and perhaps appreciation for her poise under pressure. Aleksander's smile tightened just slightly, but he recovered quickly.

"A fair observation," he acknowledged. "Though in vampire society, our nature demands a more communal understanding of relationships. The exchange of blood is both intimate and political, both personal and social. It affects not just those involved, but also the broader community's understanding of power dynamics and social structures."

"Perhaps," Kate conceded, keeping herself composed while recognizing the trap he was setting. "But that doesn't answer my fundamental question. Why should my choice, which the protégée designation explicitly grants me, be exercised here, now, at your direction rather than in private? At my discretion, following my own timeline?"

The counter-challenge was subtle but unmistakable, shifting the focus from her relationship with Devon to Aleksander's presumption in demanding this public demonstration. Devon remained silent beside her, but she felt his approval of her approach.

Aleksander's expression flickered briefly, a hint of frustration quickly masked by his usual smooth confidence. "Transparency," he replied after a moment's consideration. "Clarity about the nature of your arrangement with Devon, for the benefit of our society's understanding and acceptance. If the protégée designation is to become a recognized alternative to traditional patronage, surely its practical implications should be clearly understood."

"I see," Kate said, her tone thoughtful rather than confrontational. "And has similar transparency been required of other relationships in vampire society? Have the humans present tonight been asked to demonstrate their submission publicly? Have the vampires been asked to justify their feeding habits to the gathering's satisfaction?"

The questions were pointed but delivered with such calm dignity that they didn't appear aggressive, merely logical extensions of Aleksander's own reasoning. A few murmurs of agreement came from the gathering, suggesting that not everyone present was aligned with Aleksander's approach. Before Aleksander could respond, Devon spoke for the first time since the challenge had been issued, his voice quiet but carrying clearly through the now-silent room.

"The protégée designation is indeed about choice," he said, his gaze steady on Aleksander. "Kate's choice to share her artistic voice under my patronage. My choice to support her development without claiming ownership of her talent or her person. And yes, her choice regarding if, when, and how she shares any aspect of herself with me, including blood."

He turned slightly to face the gathering more directly, his posture straight, his expression dignified rather than defensive. "That choice is the fundamental distinction between the protégée relationship and traditional Pet designations. Not a semantic evasion, Aleksander, but a substantive difference in how we approach the connection between vampire and human."

The statement was clear, unapologetic, and a direct counter to Aleksander's implication that the protégée designation was merely a convenient fiction. Kate felt a surge of pride in Devon's principled stance, in his willingness to defend their relationship on its own terms rather than according to traditional expectations.

Aleksander's expression hardened slightly, though his voice stayed smooth. "A noble sentiment," he acknowledged. "Still, one wonders if it is entirely practical. Vampires need blood, after all. If not from a designated companion, then where? Random humans? Blood banks? Each option carries risks and complications that traditional arrangements aim to minimize."

His implication was clear: Devon's arrangement with Kate was unsustainable, meaning the natural order of vampire-human relationships would eventually reassert itself, regardless of their principled stance. Before Devon could reply, Kate stepped in, her voice clear and steady.

"Perhaps the question isn't whether vampires need blood," she suggested, "but whether that need must be met through ownership rather than partnership. Whether tradition must dictate practice or whether new approaches might better serve both vampires and humans in today's world."

Her words resonated with several vampires present, especially those who had brought human companions without traditional collars. Eliana, near the edge of the gathering, nodded slightly, showing her approval. Aleksander noticed the shift in the room's atmosphere and realized his challenge might backfire if he pushed this philosophical point further.

With the practiced adaptability that had served him well for centuries, he pivoted smoothly. "Interesting philosophical questions," he conceded. "Ones worthy of further discussion in our society. But perhaps we've drifted too far into abstraction. Let me be more direct."

Now fully facing Devon, he shed any pretense of casual inquiry. "I challenge your claim to Katherine Morgan as a protégée," he stated formally, his voice heavy with the weight of centuries-old tradition. "I offer myself as an alternative patron, with terms to be negotiated directly with her, according to her choice as the protégée designation requires."

The declaration sent shockwaves through the small gathering. This was no longer just a philosophical debate; it was a formal challenge to Devon's relationship with Kate, a direct attempt to separate them using the principles of choice and consent they had been defending.

Devon remained composed, but Kate sensed the cold anger simmering beneath his controlled exterior. "The protégée designation gives Kate the right to choose her patron," he replied carefully. "But it does not obligate her to entertain alternatives, especially when offered under such staged circumstances."

"Unless," Aleksander countered smoothly, "the protégée designation is merely a convenient fiction, as I suggested earlier. If it truly represents what you claim, a relationship based on choice rather than ownership, then surely Ms Morgan should be free to consider other options, other potential patrons who might better serve her artistic development."

The trap was elegantly set. Devon had to either acknowledge Kate's right to consider Aleksander's offer and potentially risking their relationship, or contradict his stance on the nature of the protégée designation, undermining their position in vampire society. Before Devon could respond, Kate stepped slightly forward, her movement deliberate and composed. The room fell silent, every eye focused on her as she prepared to speak.

"The protégée designation does grant me choice," she stated clearly. "Including the choice of when, where, and with whom I discuss potential patronage. This public challenge does not obligate me to negotiate or consider alternatives on demand, like a commodity at auction."

She turned to face Aleksander directly, meeting his gaze with confidence. "If you to want to discuss potential patronage, Aleksander, you should start by respecting my agency instead of trying to manipulate it for political gain. True choice cannot be coerced, even through social pressure or public spectacle."

The directness of her response momentarily caught Aleksander off guard. He quickly recovered, his smile returning but not reaching his eyes. "Well said," he acknowledged. "Yet I wonder if your... attachment to Devon clouds your judgment about what would best serve your artistic development. Sometimes we get so comfortable with familiar arrangements that we overlook better alternatives."

"My attachment to Devon," Kate replied evenly, "is part of my judgment, not a cloud over it. The patron-protégée relationship is not just transactional, it involves trust, understanding, and a fit between vision and values. These are crucial factors in my choice, and they can't be replicated through better offers or more appealing terms."

Devon stepped closer to her, their united front now both physical and philosophical. "Kate has made her choice. A choice the protégée designation gives her the right to make and keep. Without coercion or manipulation."

Aleksander studied them for a long moment, calculating his next response. The room remained silent, tension crackling in the air as the assembled vampires and humans waited to see how this confrontation would end.

Finally, Aleksander inclined his head slightly, acknowledging their position without conceding his own. "For now," he said, the two words suggesting that this issue was not resolved, just postponed. "I suspect circumstances may change and perspectives may shift. The offer remains open, Ms Morgan, should you ever find yourself… reconsidering your options."

He turned back to the rest of the gathering, seamlessly resuming the role of gracious host. "A stimulating discussion," he declared. "One that highlights the complexities of our evolving society and the relationships within it. Please, enjoy the rest of the evening. There is music in the adjacent room, and refreshments of exceptional quality available for anyone who wants them."

With that, he moved away, effectively concluding the public confrontation. The gathering began to break apart, with people forming smaller groups and conversations resuming, now mostly focused on what they had just witnessed.

Devon took Kate's hand, a subtle gesture of support and connection. "You were extraordinary," he said quietly, his voice meant just for her.

"We were," Kate corrected, gently squeezing his hand. "Together."

They stayed at the gathering for another hour, maintaining composed dignity as they interacted with guests. Some were genuinely interested in the philosophical questions raised by the confrontation, others barely concealing their curiosity about the personal dynamics they. Throughout, they presented a united front, neither defensive nor aggressive, but simply secure in the choices they had made and the relationship they were building.

When they finally took their leave, Aleksander saw them to the door personally, his manner once again the gracious host though his eyes remained calculating, assessing. "An enlightening evening," he said as they prepared to depart. "I hope you found it as clarifying as I did."

"Illuminating in many ways," Devon replied neutrally. "Though perhaps not in the ways you intended."

Aleksander's smile tightened slightly, the only indication that Devon's observation had struck home. "Until next time," he said, the words carrying both promise and threat. "I have a feeling our paths will cross again soon. The conversation is far from concluded."

"Perhaps," Devon acknowledged. "Though its terms may not be yours to dictate."

With that, they departed, maintaining their dignity and composure until they were safely in the car and moving away from Aleksander's residence. Only then did Kate feel the tension begin to leave her body, the strain of the evening's confrontation finally showing in the slight trembling of her hands.

Devon noticed immediately, taking her hands in his, his touch gentle but grounding. "You were incredible," he said, his voice warm with genuine admiration. "Few humans, or vampires, for that matter, would have handled Aleksander's challenge with such grace and clarity."

"It was more intense than I expected," Kate admitted, allowing herself to acknowledge the stress now that they were alone. "More direct, more public. He really was trying to separate us in front of everyone."

"He miscalculated," Devon observed, a hint of satisfaction in his tone. "He expected either compliance with his demand for demonstration, which would have undermined your agency, or refusal, which would have suggested distance between us. Your response, questioning the premise of his challenge rather than simply accepting or rejecting it, caught him off guard."

Kate nodded, understanding the layers of the confrontation more clearly now that it was behind them. "He's not finished, though," she said. "That was clear in his parting words."

"No," Devon agreed, his expression growing more serious. "Tonight was merely the opening move in what I suspect will be a more extended campaign. Aleksander rarely abandons a goal once set, particularly when it involves both desire and strategic advantage."

"And how do we respond?" Kate pressed.

"Together," Devon replied simply, echoing their earlier exchange. "We maintain our united front, our mutual respect, our commitment to defining our relationship on our own terms rather than according to tradition or external pressure."

Kate nodded, drawing strength from his steady presence beside her. "Together," she agreed, the word carrying all the weight of their shared experiences, their growing bond, their determination to forge a path that honored both their differences and their connection.

As the car continued its journey through the night toward the sanctuary of the estate, Kate found herself thinking of how far they had come from their beginning—from captivity to choice, from fear to trust, from isolation to partnership. Whatever challenges Aleksander might present in the days and weeks ahead, she felt confident that the foundation they had built would withstand them.

Not because their relationship was perfect or without complications, but because it was genuine, founded on mutual respect, strengthened through shared vulnerability, defined by their own choices rather than external expectations or traditions.

The estate appeared in the distance, its lights welcoming in the darkness. Kate leaned against Devon's shoulder, drawing comfort from his presence as they returned to the sanctuary they had created together. A home they would now need to defend against Aleksander's determined efforts to breach its walls.

But tonight, they had proven something important to themselves, to Aleksander, and to vampire society at large. They had shown that their relationship was not a convenient fiction or a temporary arrangement, but a genuine partnership built on choice, respect, and love. Whatever came next, they would face it with that knowledge, that strength, that unshakable foundation of trust and commitment.

Together.

Chapter 16

The candlelight changed Devon's bedroom into a warm and inviting space. A gentle rain tapped against the windows, making a calming sound that felt timeless. This was similar to the man whose bed Kate now occupied.

They lay together, sheets tangled around them, their bodies close in the cozy aftermath of desire. Devon's fingers traced lazy patterns along Kate's bare shoulder, gently following the curve of her collarbone. Kate's own hand rested on his chest, feeling the slow, steady heartbeat that required conscious effort on his part, a human gesture he maintained for her benefit.

"What are you thinking?" Devon asked, his voice soft in the dimness.

Kate smiled, turning her head to press a kiss against his shoulder. "That's my line," she teased. "You're usually the contemplative one."

"Perhaps you're rubbing off on me," he replied, his fingers continuing their gentle exploration, trailing down her arm. "But you didn't answer the question."

Kate was silent for a moment, considering. "I was thinking about time," she said finally. "How differently we experience it. For me, these past months have been transformative. A significant chapter of my life. For you, they must seem like barely a moment in your existence."

Devon shifted slightly, propping himself up on one elbow to look at her more directly. His expression was thoughtful. "Time isn't just about how long it lasts," he said. "It's also about its meaning. Some centuries go by in a blur of sameness. Meanwhile, certain moments and connections stand out clearly, no matter how short they are."

His hand moved to cup her cheek, his touch infinitely gentle despite the strength she knew he possessed. "These months with you have been more meaningful, more vivid, than decades of my existence before you entered it."

"Even the difficult parts?" she asked, thinking of her escape attempt, of Aleksander's challenge, of the complex navigation of vampire society they had undertaken together.

"Especially those," Devon confirmed, his thumb brushing lightly across her lower lip. "Immortality's greatest curse is not the loss of those we care for, though that is burden enough. It's the gradual dulling of experience, the creeping sameness that makes centuries blur together in memory."

His eyes, ancient and yet somehow youthful in their current warmth, held hers with an intensity that still took her breath away at times. "You have made me feel again, Kate. Not just desire or affection, but the full spectrum of emotion I had forgotten was possible. Worry when you attempted escape. Fear when Aleksander issued his challenge. Hope when you chose to stay despite having the choice to leave."

Kate reached up, her fingers tracing the contours of his face. She felt his strong jawline, high cheekbones, and the slight crease between his brows that showed when he was deep in thought. Features that had once seemed foreign in their perfection now felt intimately familiar and beloved for their uniqueness.

"And what about now?" she asked softly, her hand sliding to the nape of his neck, drawing him closer. "What are you feeling now?"

In answer, Devon lowered his head, his lips meeting hers in a kiss that began gently but quickly deepened, carrying all the emotion words couldn't fully express. Kate responded in kind, her body arching against his, her free hand trailing down the smooth plane of his back.

When they separated, he gently rested his forehead against hers. "Gratitude," he whispered against her lips. "Wonder, desire. A kind of… reverence I had forgotten was possible."

Kate smiled, running her fingers through his hair. "Reverence?" she repeated, playfully teasing him, but she appreciated his sincerity. "That's quite a word for what we were just doing."

A smile flickered on Devon's lips, rare and precious in its genuine warmth. "Is it?" he asked. "Acknowledging something sacred, something worthy of deep respect and appreciation. What better word for this connection we've found against all odds?"

The simple poetry of his perspective moved Kate unexpectedly, bringing a slight sheen of tears to her eyes. "Sometimes I forget how beautiful your perspective can be, how centuries of existence have given you a way of seeing things differently."

Devon's expression softened, understanding replacing concern. "And sometimes," he countered, "I forget how your human perspective—the precious brevity of your existence, the intensity with which you experience each moment—illuminates aspects of life I had ceased to notice."

His hand moved to her waist, drawing her closer against him, skin against skin in the candlelit dimness. "We balance each other," he observed. "Your passion and immediacy. My patience and perspective. Your artistic vision. My historical context."

"A perfect complementary pair," Kate agreed, her hand sliding up his chest to rest over his heart. "Though I'm not sure vampire society sees it that way."

Devon's expression grew more serious, though his touch remained gentle as his fingers traced the curve of her hip. "Vampire society has existed for millennia by resisting change," he said. "But change comes nonetheless, whether welcomed or not. Perhaps what exists between us is part of that inevitable evolution."

"Evolution," Kate repeated thoughtfully. "From captor and captive to… what we are now."

"And what are we now?" Devon asked. "How would you define what exists between us, Kate?"

Kate considered the question seriously, her fingers continuing their gentle exploration of his chest, his shoulders, the strong column of his neck. This intimate conversation during their physical closeness had become characteristic of their relationship.

"Partners," she said finally. "Not equal in power or lifespan or experience, but equal in respect. In choice. In the willingness to see and be seen, to understand and be understood."

Devon nodded slowly, his hand moving up her side, across her ribs, to cup her breast with gentle appreciation. "Partners," he echoed, testing the word. "I like that."

Kate's breath caught slightly at his touch, her body responding with the familiar warmth that his proximity always evoked. "Though at the moment," she murmured, her own hand sliding lower down his torso, "I'm less interested in definitions and more interested in… demonstration."

Devon's smile took on a different quality now, desire darkening his eyes as he responded to her touch. "As ever," he said, his voice dropping to a lower register that sent a shiver through her, "I find your artistic sensibilities impeccable. Show, don't tell, isn't that the writer's maxim?"

"Something like that," Kate agreed, her smile turning mischievous as she shifted their positions, pushing Devon gently onto his back and moving to straddle him. As she leaned down to kiss him, Kate felt deeply at peace. They had found a bond that respected her humanity and his immortality, against all odds.

* * *

The following afternoon Kate walked the grounds of the estate alone, enjoying the fresh air and sunshine after the previous night's spring rain. The carefully tended flower beds were bursting with early blooms, the air filled with the scent of damp earth.

Devon was in his daytime rest, the heavy stone slab sealed over his sleeping chamber, protecting him from the sunlight that Kate now basked in. These daylight hours had once been her only escape from his presence. Now, they were simply a natural rhythm of their life together, her time for solitude while he slept, balanced by their shared evenings.

She followed the winding path through the formal gardens, past the fire pit where she had once fallen asleep only to awaken with her head in Devon's lap. She passed the music pavilion where he played piano for her on clear evenings. Each location held memories now, the estate transformed from prison to home through the alchemy of time and changing perspective.

Without conscious intention, Kate found herself walking toward the perimeter of the property, following a path she hadn't taken in weeks. The high stone walls that had once represented her confinement came into view, solid and imposing against the blue spring sky.

As she rounded a bend in the path, something unexpected caught her eye—something that made her steps falter and then stop completely.

The gate was open.

Not just unlocked, but standing wide open, the heavy wrought iron swung inward to reveal the country road beyond, dappled with sunlight filtering through the trees that lined it. Freedom, unguarded and unimpeded, just steps away.

Kate stood frozen, staring at the open gate with a complex mixture of emotions washing through her. This had to be deliberate, either a test or a statement of trust. Devon never left the gate open, yet here it was, open and unattended, offering a choice that Kate had once dreamed of, but now found herself unexpectedly conflicted about.

She moved closer, taking slow and careful steps, until she stood at the edge of the estate and the world outside. From this spot, she could see the road stretching away, curving out of sight among the trees. It led eventually to the village, to Budapest, to airports, train stations, and all the connections that could take her back to New York, to her old life, and to the freedom she had once craved.

Kate closed her eyes and felt the spring breeze on her face. It carried the scent of wildflowers from beyond the wall. She could walk through right now. Devon was in his daytime sleep, unable to stop her. By the time he woke at sunset, she could be miles away, her trail cold, her escape complete.

The thought brought no surge of excitement, no relief, only a hollow ache in her chest that surprised her.

She opened her eyes again, turning to look back at the estate spread out below her, the gardens she had come to love, the studio where she had created some of her best work. Beyond them, the main house has graceful architecture. It includes the library where they spent hours talking, the gallery where Devon collected centuries of art that inspired him, and the chamber where they slept closely together.

Not a prison anymore. A home. Their home.

Kate turned back to the open gate, to the road beyond that represented the freedom she had once been willing to risk everything for. The choice before her was no longer about escape versus captivity. It was about two different kinds of freedom—the freedom of independence, of returning to her solitary existence in New York, versus the freedom she had found with Devon, the freedom to be fully herself, understood and accepted, challenged and supported.

She took a step forward, standing directly in the gateway now, one foot on either side of the threshold. The symbolic weight of the position wasn't lost on her; poised between two worlds, two futures, two versions of herself.

If she left now, what would Devon think when he awakened to find her gone? Would he search for her, or would he respect her choice and let her go? Would he understand that her departure wasn't a rejection of him but a reclaiming of the autonomy that had been taken from her at the beginning of their story?

And if she stayed, what did that mean for her future? For their future together? How would they continue to navigate the complexities of vampire society, of Aleksander's continued interest, of the fundamental differences in their lifespans and experiences?

Kate stood motionless in the gateway, the breeze lifting her hair, the sun warm on her face, the choice before her as clear and as complex as any she had ever faced. Freedom had been her goal for so long that the concept had become almost abstract, a principle rather than a practical reality. Now, confronted with its concrete manifestation, she found herself questioning what freedom truly meant to her now, after everything that had happened.

Was it the lack of constraint? The chance to go where she wanted, when she wanted? Or was it something deeper, the freedom to be completely herself, known and understood, to create a life based on choice rather than circumstance?

The open gate stood there, waiting and indifferent to her inner conflict.

Beyond it, the road extended, providing one kind of freedom. Behind her, the estate unfolded in all its beauty and complexity, offering another.

Kate took a deep breath, the scent of spring filling her lungs, the moment of decision crystallizing around her like amber preserving a perfect instant in time.

The choice was hers alone to make.

Thank You For Reading

If you enjoyed reading *The Pet*, please consider leaving a review!

https://www.amazon.com/gp/product/B0FHH6QXZL

About the Author

Samantha Beneke is a South African-born writer who now calls New Zealand home. With a background in Media & Communications, she has spent her career crafting compelling narratives across multiple platforms, from digital marketing campaigns to literary publications.

Samantha's writing journey began early, earning recognition as a published teenage poet through several publications with the prestigious Douglas Livingstone Poetry competition in South Africa. Her talent for weaving words into powerful emotional experiences has continued throughout her career, with numerous magazine articles and online publications showcasing her versatility as a writer.

"The Pet" marks Samantha's debut into novel writing, where she explores themes of trust, choice, power, and transformative love through the lens of dark paranormal romance.

When she's not writing, Samantha continues to work in digital marketing, always seeking new ways to connect with audiences and tell stories that matter.

To follow her work and receive updates visit samanthabenekeromanceauthor.com

https://www.tiktok.com/@samantha_beneke
https://www.instagram.com/supernaturalromanceauthor/
https://www.facebook.com/supernaturalromanceauthor/

Other Works By Samantha

Don't miss the next book in the series!

THE CAPTIVE HEARTS SERIES

- The Partner - Book Two
- The One (releasing 31 March 2026)

9 780473 753122